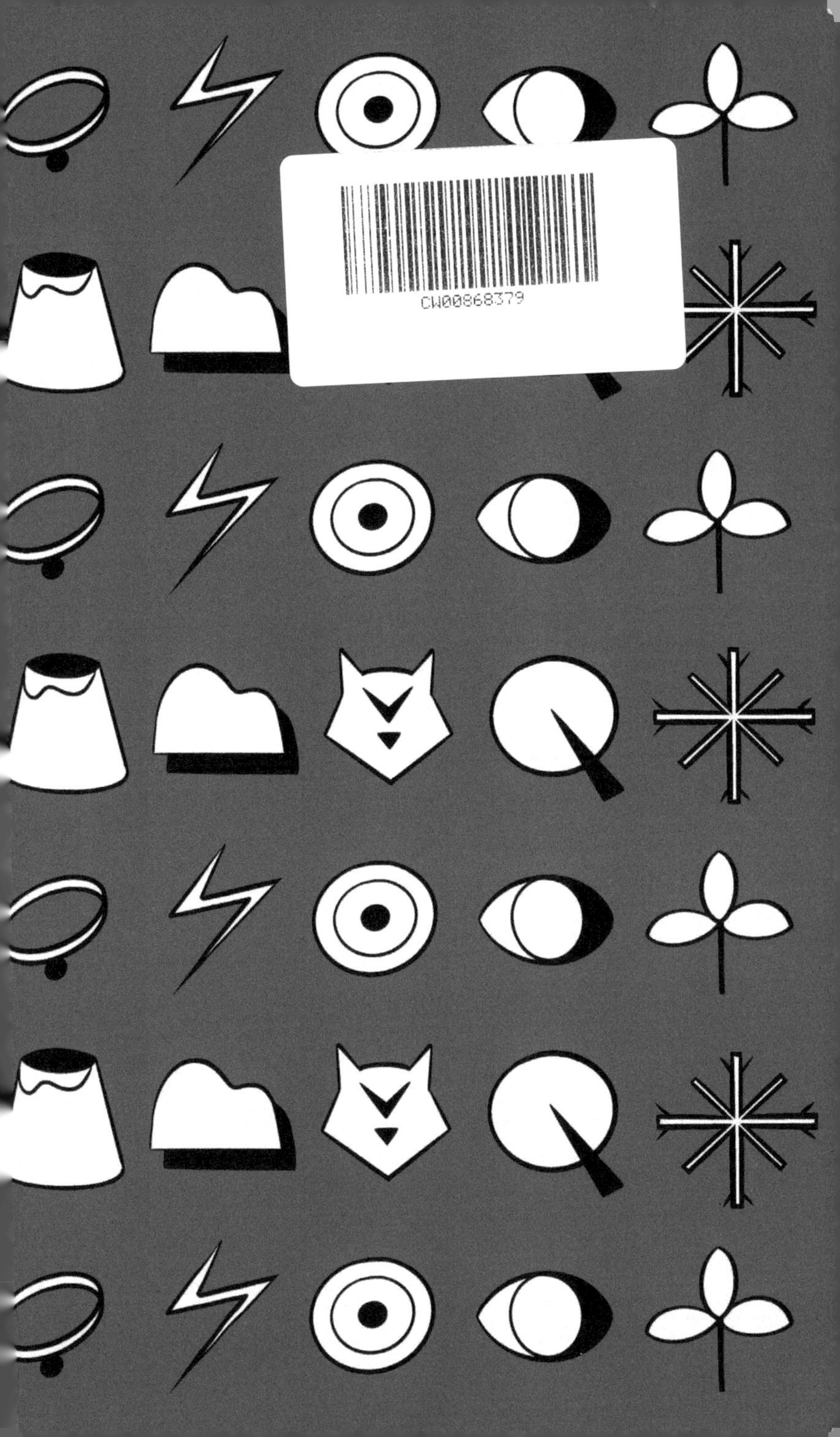
CW00868379

Story Makers Press

Published by Story Makers Press
Part of The Story Makers Company at Leeds Beckett University
Carnegie Hall, Headingley Campus, Leeds LS6 3QW

First published in 2021
Written by Tom Dobson
World building by Lisa Stephenson
Editing by Ana Arêde
Illustrated by Bethany Kippax

Set in Nobel, 13 pt
Designed and typeset by Samuel Baker
Printed and bound in the UK

ISBN: 9781916437579

2 4 6 8 10 9 7 5 3 1

This book is produced from independently certified FSC® paper.

THE STORY MAKERS

The children of Stephen Longfellow Academy
Lisa Stephenson
Tom Dobson
Ana Sanches de Arêde
Bethany Kippax
Samuel Baker

Mentors:
Mark Oliver
Anjan Sarkar

INTERGALACTIC SUPERHERO SCHOOL

JOURNEY TO PLANET EARTH

WELCOME TO SUPERHERO SCHOOL

On behalf of the Alliance, welcome to the Intergalactic Superhero School. For those of you from Dark Planet, it is my **extra-special** pleasure to welcome you here. You are, as everyone will know, our first ever Dark Planet recruits! Believe me when I say how happy we are that you are here.

My name is Professor Mark Wells, but before I retired as a superhero I was known as Lightning. Now, I know you've come to hear about Wolf. But my story and Wolf's are entwined. There are many myths and rumours that circulate about him and what happened all those years ago. About our infamous mission to Planet Earth. About how he betrayed the Alliance. About how he betrayed his own people.

I'm pleased to see that members of the Intergalactic Media have joined us for this event. I will not disappoint you. I will set the record straight once and for all. I will tell you the true story about Wolf and the mission to Planet Earth.

But it's important to start from the beginning. You need to understand how different things were back then. The planets and the galaxies in the Alliance were not as peaceful and cooperative as they are now. Even though we now have climate catastrophes to resolve and computer-generated viruses to control, we work together. And while there's the occasional evil act of terrorism which we have to counter, we know these could be carried out by any of the planets in the Alliance.

But, back then, we were at war with Dark Planet. The purpose of the Intergalactic Superhero School was very different when I first joined, when I sat ready for my first instruction.

Back then, we were known only by the name of our power and were supposed to forget our original names. It felt weird. Like we had become someone else. You can all keep your own names now. The superpower names that you give each other will be nicknames, just for fun. Our understanding of the brain and emotional wellbeing is a lot more advanced now and we know that for you to execute your powers for the greatest good of the Alliance you must feel happy and secure about who you are.

Another big difference was that most planets and space stations had various protection measures in place. Planet Earth was the notable exception. It always lagged behind the rest of the planets in terms of security. That's why we succeeded in travelling there on our first mission. But I'll get to the part where Wolf came face-to-face with Crocodile later.

You will know that our school was surrounded by a security circle – an invisible forcefield put in place to keep our enemies out. Sat here amongst the new recruits we have budding superheroes from all planets, including Dark Planet. But, back then, some of you would have been considered our enemies. Indeed, the Alliance were so fearful of what the people of Dark Planet and their leader Crocodile might do that they imprisoned Dark Planet in a ring of fire. At the time, it seemed a reasonable measure to take.

BOY ON THE MOON

I'll start at the beginning. My beginning and my lonely childhood. I don't remember having parents and I didn't have any siblings or any friends either. I didn't have anyone to talk to. It was just me, a small boy, and my five-legged dog, Fiver, alone on a moon. When the scouts from the Intergalactic Superhero School brought me here and I was told at the security circle checkpoint to forget my past, there wasn't much to forget. People ask me how I ended up on that moon. But, to be honest, until I came here, I'd never even thought about it.

No, the truth is that I just accepted my lot. My house was a rusty shelter made from a broken metal shell. I had one possession – a book called *The War of the Worlds*, about an alien invasion. I knew my name was Mark because it said 'This book belongs to Mark' inside the book.

It was cold on the moon. Most of the time the only water was frozen in the craters. The rock itself was dusty, grey and hard. One of my earliest memories is being aware of a buzzing in my fingertips, a strange and uncomfortable feeling like pins and needles, but worse. I shook my hands instinctively and watched with surprise as thin white lines shot from my finger and singed poor Fiver's furry back.

I didn't really embrace my superpower at first, probably for fear of hurting Fiver, but also because I didn't really understand what it was. The electricity would build up to such a point that my hands became so uncomfortable I just had to shake them. It wasn't long, however, before we learnt to enjoy the lightning. Fiver and I would go out for long walks and I'd hold back, feeling the lightning build up in my fingers before unleashing its power on a boulder or a crater. We would watch in amazement as the rocks were blasted up into the air before descending with a mighty crash, sending plumes of dust everywhere. Fiver's tail would wag at the very sight of this destruction. Before the dust even settled he'd scamper off to find a rock to bring back to me.

So that became our life on the moon. Going out on walks to blast rocks and craters before coming back to read *The War of the Worlds* again. That is, until they found me.

I'd been saving up my power for over a week with the idea of causing maximum destruction and Fiver and I had marched excitedly to a giant crater to blast it to smithereens. The result was impressive, but it caused such a disturbance that the scouts from the school saw it from their spaceship. Fiver was still fetching rocks when the spaceship started to descend, blowing all the dust back up into the air before landing right beside us.

Fiver barked wildly at the sight of it, fearing we were under some kind of alien attack, urging me to release my lightning on the small craft. But my power was spent, so when two scouts in silver spacesuits emerged and walked towards us, we had no choice but to wait and see what they wanted.

They took off their helmets and smiled at me, one of them bending down in an attempt to stroke Fiver who was still barking wildly.

'We come in peace,' the taller one said.

I nodded. It was the first time I'd heard anyone speak but, somehow, I understood what her words meant and I knew that these strangers weren't going to attack us.

'We're from the Intergalactic Superhero School,' the other one said, giving up on trying to stroke Fiver. 'We saw what you did with that crater and we think you have what it takes to become a superhero.'

I'd lived about as sheltered a life as it was possible to live. Everything I knew about the universe I knew from one book and my life on the moon with Fiver. So, of course, I knew nothing about superheroes or the school. But what I did know was that it felt overwhelmingly good to be with other people. People who talked the way people did in the book. After years of living alone on a rock they could have been offering me anything, a ten-year intergalactic prison sentence, and I would have taken it!

'Count me in,' I said, smiling back at them. 'On one condition: Fiver comes too.'

SECURITY CIRCLE CHECKPOINT

They exchanged looks.

The taller one said, 'It would be unusual.'

'We can't just leave the dog here,' the smaller one said. 'Look at this place! How did you end up here anyway?'

I shrugged my shoulders.

The taller one pointed to the broken shell of my shelter. 'I'd say he crash landed here.'

At first, I didn't understand. I didn't crash land here. I lived here. This was my home.

The smaller one walked towards my shelter and ran his silver gloves across its broken silver surface. 'One of those old Rover spacecrafts,' he said. 'Decommissioned about ten years ago due to deceleration problems when landing.'

I looked at the shelter, the only home I knew, and saw it for what it really was: an old spaceship that had crash landed with me and Fiver on board.

'But, why can't I remember the crash?' I asked them. 'I would have been too young to have been travelling on my own in a spaceship, even with a dog to keep me company?'

The taller scout lowered her head and gently put her hand on my back. It felt weird and I backed away from her instinctively.

'Poor fella,' said the shorter one, bending down to pat Fiver. 'Looks like your parents must have used the ejector button before it crashed. Of course you can bring your dog.'

I felt numb as I got into their spaceship. My mind racing to try and remember my parents. But I could remember nothing. The crash must have been so forceful, I later realised, that my memory of everything beforehand was wiped. Amnesia is the medical term for it. I imagined them in the failing spacecraft, pressing the buttons, trying to get all us all out to safety... Their ejector seats working, but mine and Fiver's for some reason getting stuck... And yet we were the ones who survived! Unless, of course, they did too...

At one point on the journey I looked out of the small window and back down at my moon. How small, grey and cold it was, I thought. I felt lonely. As if Fiver and I were smaller than ever. Insignificant specks in the massive galaxy.

'Try not to look,' the taller scout said softly. 'It's common to feel strange when you first leave your home. You'll get used to it though.'

The motion of the spaceship eventually sent me to sleep. When I woke, the taller scout announced we were approaching the security circle.

I looked out of the window but couldn't see anything.

'It's an invisible forcefield, made of energy, that repels unwelcome guests,' she explained. 'We go in through the checkpoint, but our enemies are kept out.'

'What happens to them?' I asked.

'Just think of what happens to your moon rocks when you blast them with your lightning!' the other scout replied, laughing.

'Well,' said the taller scout, laughing along with her friend, 'this is the end of the road for us. We're heading back to scour the galaxies for more superheroes. It's been a pleasure meeting you, Lightning.'

'Lightning?' I asked quizzically. 'My name's Mark.'

'Not for much longer,' the other scout said. The spaceship slowed down and, as the security circle opened, I could see the forcefield, the entrance like giant jaws ready to swallow us whole. 'They'll explain all of that to you in due course.'

'And they might find you have another superpower and give you another name,' the taller scout added. 'But we're generally right about these things.'

'Yes,' said the shorter one proudly. 'Nine times out of ten we're right about these things.'

I'd only known them a few hours, but as Fiver and I stepped out into the checkpoint I felt a sudden sadness in the pit of my stomach. I didn't even know their names but they were the only people I'd ever known. I didn't want them to go.

'Hey, wait a minute!' I shouted after them. But it was too late. The doors of their spaceship had closed and they were heading back out into space.

The checkpoint was a series of metal rooms, most of them bare, with high, dark ceilings. On each of the walls was the emblem of the Alliance – a white ring surrounding all of the major planets. My moon, of course, was not included.

Fiver and I were greeted by a person wearing a green medical outfit, a mask over their face and their hair in a kind of shower cap. They weren't very welcoming, ushering us into a room with showers in it, before motioning for me to take off my clothes. They took them and put them in an empty sack.

That felt weird, undressing in front of a stranger and peeling off the clothes I'd worn most of my life. I didn't smell too great, I'm not ashamed to say. The person turned on the showers at the back of the room. Fiver and I had never seen so much water, and for a moment we forgot where we were and started splashing each other, having a great time.

When the water went off, a different door slid open and another person in a similar outfit led me to a table where I was told to lie down. I didn't know it at the time, but this was the medical room. I didn't like it one bit and, I could tell Fiver didn't either. It took three of them to restrain him and seeing the fear in his eyes made me thrash too. It wasn't long before four more of them in white suits came to restrain me.

None of the people spoke. They took blood from us with various syringes but I guess they didn't find anything wrong because soon they were gone and another door opened. Fiver was still shaking from the medical examination so I carried him through. Once inside, I found a brand-new blue oufit waiting for me on a chair. I set Fiver down and put the uniform on. I didn't like the feel of the material against my skin. It was rough, different from what I was used to, but Fiver started barking appreciatively at the sight of me. He almost seemed back to his old self.

Another door opened and it was in the next room that I met a superhero whose name you will all know. Freeze. What a legend he was to become! The one-and-only future saviour of Planet Earth! He'd been picked up just before I had, found by different scouts on a moon at the outer reaches of this galaxy. Despite what they say about his cold touch, he was one of the friendliest superheroes you could ever meet.

He held out his formidable hand for me to shake. 'I'm Freeze,' he said.

'Mark,' I said, holding my own hand out only slightly, reluctant for him to take it. But take it he did. 'Ow!' I shouted, reeling in pain. Not just from the strength of his grip but from the temperature. Freeze was, as you would expect, quite literally freezing.

'You haven't been in there yet, have you Mark?' Freeze

said, gesturing to a wall. The door it contained was invisible at that point.

'Not yet,' I said. 'Why do you ask?'

Freeze smiled. A friendly smile, but a smile that looked in danger of cracking his chiselled face in two. 'You'll see,' was all he said.

CHAPTER 04
THE ROOM OF NEW BEGINNINGS

'Welcome to the Room of New Beginnings,' the receptionist greeted us without a smile. He was wearing the standard blue uniform and was reading from some papers on a clipboard. 'You are... Lightning,' he said, matter-of-factly.

'Yes,' I began, 'but my real name—'

'We're not worried about that here,' he replied. 'From now on, you are Lightning. You must forget your previous name and you must forget your previous life. Here you will learn how to become your superpower. It is the only way you will be able to serve the Alliance.'

He spoke so authoritatively that I didn't dare question him. I realised I wasn't too precious about my name anyway. I thought that I was called Mark because of the book. But, try as I might, I could not remember my parents or anyone else ever calling me Mark.

'And this is?' the receptionist asked, pointing dismissively at poor Fiver.

'My dog, Fiver,' I said, trying to sound as proud of Fiver as possible.

'And does your dog have a superpower?'

'Not that I know of,' I replied. 'But he does have five legs.'

The man noted something down on his clipboard. 'They shouldn't have let him in here.'

'I said I wouldn't come without him,' I told him firmly. 'Where we live it's just us, you see. A moon—'

'We're not interested in that here,' he interrupted me again. 'As I said, you must forget your past. Since the dog is here, he can stay. From what I read in your notes, your power is a strong one. It would be churlish to lose you over a dog.'

The receptionist pointed to a light bulb on a table. 'I'm going to ask you some questions, Lightning. If the bulb turns green, you have answered correctly. If it turns red, you have not.'

'What does that mean?' I asked.

He ignored me and instead began asking questions about Dark Planet.

'Are you from Dark Planet?'

'I've never heard of Dark Planet.'

Red light.

'Answer the question: are you from Dark Planet?'

'No. I'm from–'

Green light.

'Do you know anyone from Dark Planet?'

'Where I'm from–'

Red light.

'Answer the question.'

'No.'

Green light.

'What are your feelings about the people of Dark Planet?'

'I don't have any feelings because I've never heard of–'

Green light.

With every answer I gave him he scribbled something down on his paper and frowned.

'What would you do if you met someone from Dark Planet?'

'I don't know.'

Red light.

My last response drew the biggest frown from my interrogator. He went on to give me a brief lesson in the history of Dark Planet. It's a history which has since been contested and corrected, but back then it was the way history was told.

'Well, Lightning,' the receptionist said matter-of-factly once again. 'Let me tell you what you would do. You would use your superpower to destroy them.'

I thought about the aliens in *The War of the Worlds*. Wasn't destroying other beings the kind of thing that only happened in books?

'The people of Dark Planet are evil,' he continued. 'They have only one aim: to destroy the Alliance and achieve intergalactic domination. Ever since Crocodile waged war on Red Planet, this has been their goal. It was why Red Planet started the Alliance in the first place. To protect us all from Dark Planet. It was why the Alliance started this school. To use all the superpowers available across our galaxy; to nurture the superheroes who will ultimately destroy Crocodile and his evil people. It's why we surrounded Dark Planet in a ring of fire.' The receptionist looked at me sternly. 'So, Lightning, what would you do if you met someone from Dark Planet?'

I had so many questions. Who was Crocodile? Where was Dark Planet? And could all of its people really be evil? But I knew from the look on his face that this wasn't the time to ask.

'I'd use my superpower to destroy them,' I told him.

Green light.

For the first time, the receptionist smiled at me. 'Welcome to the Intergalactic Superhero School, Lightning.'

WOLF'S EYES

It wasn't long before a spaceship took us from the security circle checkpoint to the superhero school itself. The school was a lot smaller back then. Each grade had to take it in turns to use one of the two simulation rooms and we didn't have this lecture theatre where we could all get together and share our knowledge.

It was just a lot more basic. The uniforms were rough on our skin, the food was unhealthy – deep fried in fat – there was no common room for us to relax in and no computer games for us to play...

I'm beginning to sound like an old fart! Forgive me. Of course, it's better now. Having over a hundred simulation rooms means that you can develop and harness your superpowers much more quickly than we were able to. Back then it took longer, and this meant that, with the exception of All Powers, we were only permitted to develop one power; to become that power. I was Lightning because of the lightning that flowed through my fingertips. Freeze was Freeze because he could freeze anything he touched. But it's possible that we have other powers. Powers that no one, not even ourselves, realised. Powers that, to this day, remain untapped.

And now, in this time of relative peace, we appreciate that powers are not the be-all and end-all. That, to be a superhero, you also need to develop your whole self. That is why you will undertake lessons in character. To become better people. To understand others. To have empathy and compassion. To be able to resolve conflict through non-violent means.

But at the time I arrived things were a lot less sophisticated. The people of Dark Planet were evil, or so we were told. Their leader, Crocodile, was the most evil, or so we were told. You have one power, they told us, and you must use it to defeat evil. To defeat Dark Planet. To defeat Crocodile.

Where was I? The small spaceship came to a halt and the door to the superhero school slid open. Fiver was reluctant to move. Wanting to help, Freeze bent down to pick him up. Poor Fiver! I'd never heard him wail so loudly before!

At reception, one of the administrators welcomed us. 'It's late,' he told us, 'so I've been asked to take you straight to your dormitory. The others will be asleep. You can meet them in the morning.' He turned to me. 'The dog will have to make do with the bottom of your bed.'

Inside the dorm were three bunks. From where we stood we could just make out that two of them were occupied by the outline of the duvets.

'Bagsy top bunk,' said Freeze, already climbing the ladder of the unoccupied bunk.

Despite the fact that my learning had been restricted to one book about an alien invasion, I'd miraculously understood most things that had been said to me that day. The word 'bagsy', however, eluded me. Freeze had already discarded his duvet to make sure he kept himself ice cold, so I didn't bother asking him what it meant. Instead, I put his duvet at the foot of my bed for Fiver and lay down to sleep.

How to describe the feeling of sleeping on a mattress after a lifetime of sleeping on rock? It felt as if my whole body was suddenly weightless, as light as a feather, as if I were being caressed softly by the length of the mattress. I could have stayed in that bed for the rest of my life!

It had been a strange day for me, to put it mildly. I'd gone from living on a rock with Fiver to meeting other people for the first time. I'd gone from realising that I had most probably been orphaned by a spacecraft crash to being here, at a superhero school, sleeping in a dormitory with five other budding young superheroes. As I began to fall asleep, everything that had happened that day flashed in and out of my mind. It wasn't a nice feeling. It felt like I was out of control. Like I didn't know who I was anymore. *Lightning. Parents I didn't know I'd had and couldn't remember. The scouts, who were the first people I had seen. This book belongs to Mark...*

Just before I drifted off, I saw the whites of two glassy eyes staring down at me from the top bunk across the room. The eyes were jet black in the middle and lit up by a searing redness. I tried to hold the stare but couldn't help blinking. After a few blinks I must have fallen asleep, Wolf's eyes watching me the whole time.

CHAPTER 06

BREAKFAST WITH THE CREW

If you'd have said to me back then that out of all the superheroes in our crew – the five in my dorm plus the three others I met the next day – the one I'd be closest to would be Wolf, I would have laughed at you. For the first two days he wouldn't even look at me! Every time I tried to catch his attention, he would look away, covering his face behind his great wave of brown hair, snarling and scraping his fingernails together. He was different at night-time, though. Wolf didn't seem to ever sleep and every night, as I drifted into blissful unconsciousness, I could feel his jet black eyes on me. I remember thinking, *Just what is your problem, Wolf?*

The others were more welcoming, though. Having struggled to get to sleep, Fiver and I were enjoying the mattress-that-wasn't-a-rock so much that we slept through the others getting up and going to the canteen for breakfast. The only reason we eventually tore ourselves from the bed was because Teleport – Tele for short – came back for us.

'Wake up, dudes!' he was saying in that chirpy way of his. 'You know what they say – breakfast is the most important meal of the day!'

I got up and Tele held out his hand for me to shake. Instinctively I moved away from him, but he grabbed my hand anyway. His felt weird and soft. Like holding a ball of cotton wool.

Tele laughed. 'You know what they say about me, Lightning?'

I shrugged my shoulders.

'That I'm not quite all here.'

I was about to ask him where the others were and where we went for breakfast, but I was too late. Before I could speak, Tele, quite literally, wasn't there.

There were about a hundred superheroes in the school at that time.

Before I had a chance to work out which table Freeze was at, three superheroes were waving and smiling and making their way from the queue for food over to us. They bent down to stroke Fiver. What they say about dogs is true: they are a great ice-breaker.

"I'm Laser," squeaked Laser in that high-pitched voice of his, flashing his piercing green eyes at me just long enough to be welcoming without doing me any damage.

"All Powers," smiled All Powers, high fiving me and saying something about how she was beginning to learn to produce lightning herself.

"And, for some reason, I'm Banana," said Banana with a friendly glint in her eye, brushing her long green hair out of her face before grabbing my hand and leading me over to the others. 'Everyone, this is Lightning and his dog, Fiver,' she said. 'Lightning, this is everyone!'

We had to sit with our class in the canteen. Our crew, the nine of us plus Fiver, were the new recruits. The first graders. I looked around the table and was amazed. Despite our blue uniforms, there was nothing uniform about the way we looked. We were all so different. There was Lava, the orange heat of her lava painfully visible beneath the thin tanned skin of her cheeks. Next to Lava was her best friend Obsidian, jet black and so straight-backed that he looked permanently uncomfortable due to his bones being the hardest of hard rock. Then there was the recognisable smile of Freeze, whose grey skin seemed to be steaming in the heat of the canteen. Tele, who had saved me from missing my first breakfast, was now at the table, always smiling, never quite there. And, at the far end of the table, was Wolf, hunched over his plate of fried eggs, his long brown hair covering his jet black eyes.

'Hi, I'm Mark,' I said. Fiver barked his hello.

'Mark?' replied Wolf gruffly, his eyes still fixed on his fried eggs. 'What kind of superpower is *Mark*?'

'He means *Lightning*,' said Banana softly. 'Apart from you and Freeze, the rest of us have had a few days to get used to our new names. Although I'm still not sure I'm happy with Banana.'

'Why are you called Banana?' I asked.

'She does this thing with plants,' Tele explained. 'She can control them. Wrap roots and vines around people. Strangle them to death.'

'But what's that go to do with bananas?' I asked.

'My point exactly!' said Banana, pretending to be put out.

'It's not for us to argue about our names,' Tele continued. 'I guess they thought that Banana sounded better than Root or Vine, and they were probably right, don't you think, dude?'

'OK,' interrupted Lava, glancing at her watch. 'Get yourself some breakfast, Lightning. Our first lesson with Professor Banks starts in a minute.'

CHAPTER 07
PROFESSOR BANKS

Lava was always punctual. When you've got lava bubbling up inside of you it must help. You always want to keep moving and you're always thinking about where you need to be next. Getting to the next place helps stop the feeling that you might explode.

I grabbed some eggs and sausages for me and Fiver and sat at the end of the table, next to Banana and opposite Wolf.

If Lava was always punctual, then Banana was always enthusiastic. She started telling me how lucky we were to have Professor Banks as our teacher. 'If it wasn't for her potions, we might not be winning in our battle against Dark Planet!'

'How so?' I asked her, explaining that my knowledge of history was limited to *The War of the Worlds*.

'Well, she's the one who caused Crocodile to lose some of the power of his bite,' Banana explained. 'Professor Banks's power is manipulating the toxins from plants. She gave Crocodile lockjaw for the best part of the week and he's never been quite the same since.'

'According to who?' asked Wolf, chewing on some fried bread, still not looking up at either of us.

'Oh, I don't know,' replied Banana brightly. '*People*. That's what people say.'

'Proof, if proof were needed, that *people* don't know anything,' Wolf said cuttingly.

As I was to soon appreciate, Wolf had a way of killing

conversations. With time, I became more adept at laughing at his surly ways – so much so that occasionally he would laugh back – but I can understand how people were put off by him.

'Sounds like a legend!' I managed to say before Lava told us all that it was time to get to class.

I'd never been in a classroom before. I didn't understand what you had to do. On that first morning, I just kept getting up and walking around with Fiver, shaking my itching hands. I wanted to bust a hole in the wall or the table. Lightning was building up in my arms and I felt like I was about to burst.

To be fair to the professor, she was patient with me. Entreating me to sit down. Telling me to sit down. Ordering me to sit down. Eventually she handed me a glass of blue liquid and said calmly, 'Lightning. You need to sit down like the rest of the class or you will leave me with no other choice than to sedate you with one of my potions.'

I couldn't tell whether she was joking or not. That was always the way with her. She had this dry sense of humour and any joke she ever made was done with a straight face.

Remembering what Banana had said about Crocodile's lockjaw, I sat down. 'I'm not thirsty at the moment, thank you, Professor.'

Once we were all settled at our desks, the professor gave us an overview of what we would be doing. 'You have all been selected because you are different from other people. They may have powers, but your powers have been identified as exceptional. Your powers are potentially superpowers. But don't be fooled. At the moment your powers are just that – potential. Your powers are rough, unformed and erratic. They come and go, and they are not yet under your full control. All of a sudden a wave of electricity, a surge of Lava, the claws of a wolf, may emerge from you, may change you, at the just the wrong moment. And at those moments when do need your powers, when you are under attack, when you need to protect yourselves, you will remain as you are now. Untransformed. Your everyday selves. Flickers of power. Or, as I said, potential.'

The professor looked beyond us, at some vague point at the back of the classroom. 'I can remember when I attended my first lesson here. It was five years after the school had been set up and I thought I knew it all. I thought I was the business! The real deal! But every potion I made was essentially just a sedative that knocked my fellow students out for different lengths of time. It took months for me to enhance my senses of touch and smell to read the different plants and refine my potion-making skills so that I could respond to the various superpowers I was trying to nullify. I learnt how to lessen the flow of electricity,' here the professor lifted her glasses and smiled at me, 'immobilise fast-moving legs, lock the jaw of Crocodile.'

I shared a knowing smile with Banana who was sat at the desk to the left of me. To hear her acknowledging that she had locked the jaw of Crocodile certainly commanded our respect.

Well, almost all of us. I glanced round at my classmates and, of course, the only one not smiling at the professor was Wolf. He was just staring impassively at his new teacher with those piercing jet black eyes of his.

The professor ignored this, but I could hear Lava and Obsidian muttering to each other behind me.

'What's the matter, Wolf?' Obsidian called.

Wolf just grunted by way of reply.

'Yes,' added Lava. 'Are you not impressed by our professor's achievement? By the look of you, anyone would have thought that locking Crocodile's jaw was a bad thing.'

The professor continued. 'For the first few weeks, in phase one, you will learn about your own superpower. You will learn about what it is now, what it can become and how you can use it against our enemies from Dark Planet.' She pointed to a poster on the wall which depicted Dark Planet surrounded by a ring of fire. 'That means you will also learn about Dark Planet. Its history, its inhabitants, its leader, Crocodile, and how you can help us move from our containment strategy to domination and one day, maybe, integration.'

With great effort, Obsidian raised his hand. 'What does integration mean, Professor Banks? I thought our purpose was crush them; to annihilate the people of Dark Planet.'

Professor Banks nodded her head slowly. 'It may well come to that, Obsidian. That's what some people in the Alliance think will happen. But there's also a chance that, when we capture Crocodile, we will find the people of Dark Planet are not all evil. Some people think – and I include myself in this – that we will be able to work with them. To extinguish the ring of fire and for Dark Planet to become members of the Alliance.' The professor smiled at us, her eyes distant and contemplative. 'But I'm getting ahead of myself. Way ahead of myself. First things first, I want you all to prepare a short presentation about your superpower.' The professor pointed at my dog. 'And, Fiver, you're included in this!'

CHAPTER 08
THE PRESENTATIONS

Most of the presentations were pretty much as you'd expect them to be. Ever the enthusiast, Banana went first and told us about how she had started pulling the vines from trees, swinging joyfully from one vine to the next through an entire forest.

'It was such fun!' she said enthusiastically. 'It wasn't long before I learnt to capture small animals by wrapping vines around them and giving them to my dad to cook for our tea. I was popular in our household, I can tell you. As I grew more powerful, I learnt that I could do the same thing with roots. Make roots appear through the surface of the earth. I'd create booby-traps and trip up my friends!'

Then Laser explained how unfortunate his timing was when he discovered his power on his first date. 'I really liked him. We were gazing at each other the way people do when they really like each other. Only we didn't get any further than that because his eyes started to sting. He closed them tight and ran to the tap to bathe them in water.'

Lava and Obsidian did their presentation together. They explained how they'd grown up as neighbours, siblings practically, and how Obsidian would always make fun of Lava. 'Hundreds of years ago, I would have been lava,' Obsidian explained, each word echoing from his mouth ever so slowly. 'But, over time, that lava cooled down and turned to stone. The hardest stone in the galaxy! It's a joke between the two of us. From an evolutionary perspective, I'm just a much more advanced version of Lava!'

Tele suddenly appeared at the front of the class and spent most of his presentation demonstrating by disappearing and then reappearing in different areas of the classroom. He said he'd first discovered his power playing hide-and-seek with his sister. 'I could hear her coming towards the cupboard where I was hiding, so I closed my eyes and willed myself to disappear. When I opened my eyes I was sat in the bath.' Tele laughed. 'I never lost a game of hide-and-seek after that!'

I told them my story about blasting craters on the moon with Fiver. When it was Fiver's turn he just started barking. Everyone except Wolf laughed and Fiver ran over to each of them in turn, his tail wagging, enjoying being stroked and patted by his new superhero friends.

'That's Fiver's power. Bringing you all together as a team,' said Professor Banks, wisely. 'I can see that Fiver will have a key role to play when it comes to phase two.'

'Phase two?' asked Banana.

'Yes, phase one is about you each developing your superpowers and phase two is about learning to work together as a crew,' the professor explained. 'That's the only way to defeat the evil of Dark Planet. To become a crew and complement each other's powers. Isn't it wonderful to have Fiver with us for that?'

Next up was All Powers. 'I have the power of All Powers,' she began nervously. 'I can do everything that each of you can do. I can create lava and become as hard as the hardest stone. I'm learning to shoot lightning, control roots and vines, disappear and reappear, be a wolf and even make potions. There is nothing that I can't do.'

'That's impressive,' the professor said thoughtfully. 'But it goes against our way of thinking here at the school. The idea here is that you maximise one of your powers, hone it, refine it, develop it to such an extent that it becomes an ultimate power. The ultimate power that will complement the powers of the crew to make you a collective force to be reckoned with.'

Poor All Powers looked embarrassed. 'But, I'm not like that, Professor,' she insisted. 'My powers just come. And whilst some are stronger than others, I know that someday I will be able to use them all.'

The professor smiled kindly at her, shaking her head ever so slightly. 'All in good time,' she told her. 'I think you need to choose a power which no one else in the crew possesses. I don't want to persuade you to be something you're not, but you could choose potions. I could help you with that. Banana can make the plants do what she wants them to do and you could extract their toxins. I could help you to become Potion.'

All Powers smiled at the professor, but I could see she felt sad and, as she sat down, Fiver ran over to her and nuzzled gently against her leg.

Freeze seemed to have stopped steaming now that he was out of the canteen and in the cooler climate of the classroom. 'I was always different from the other people on my planet,' Freeze began in that easy manner of his. 'The planet was warm, you see, so I felt like I was always about to melt, and this weakened me. Back home, they had me down as a sickly child, but here I feel rejuvenated, as if I can be my true self.'

For some reason this made me feel better about myself, knowing that Freeze was happy to leave his people behind. And All Powers seemed to speak for all of us when she said, 'Perhaps our powers mean that sometimes we can feel like we don't belong. Perhaps we can belong together, Freeze.'

Last up was Wolf. He wasn't nervous, more reluctant, and he made sure his wave of hair covered his jet black eyes for the whole of his short speech. 'I am part man, part wolf,' he began. 'I smell out creatures and rip them to shreds within seconds. My power is greatest at night,' he finished.

'Tell us – where are you from, Wolf?' said the professor.

I could see Wolf scratching his thighs with his long nails. 'You wouldn't have heard of it, Professor,' Wolf tersely replied, already on his way back to his seat.

Fiver scampered over to him, but Wolf just flicked him away with the back of his hairy hand.

'I bet he's from Dark Planet,' I heard Obsidian mutter behind me.

The professor must have heard him too. 'It's a common misconception,' she said loudly, looking directly at Obsidian, 'that only people from Dark Planet can have animal superpowers. But that's not true. Granted, Crocodile is from Dark Planet and he has crocodile powers, but so many of our own superheroes have animal powers too. Why, in this very school we have Bird, Snake, Rhino and Dog, to name but a few. And, of course, our very own Wolf.'

'If you say so, Professor,' muttered Obsidian.

'I do say so, Obsidian!' the professor insisted. 'Because it's precisely this kind of ignorant thinking – that the people of Dark Planet are animals and that the people of the Alliance are somehow more refined – that will ensure the Intergalactic Battle will never end.'

The professor removed her glasses and rubbed her eyes. 'Well,' she concluded, 'I think you are an amazing group of superheroes with the potential to become one of the greatest crews. And, who knows, perhaps one day you will be the crew to defeat Crocodile and liberate Dark Planet to bring peace to the Alliance for ever. Time for lunch now, but after that it'll be our turn in the simulation room.'

CHAPTER 09

THE SIMULATION ROOM

Despite his rudeness to Fiver, Banana and I tried our best to talk to Wolf over lunch. I wondered whether his upbringing had been as lonely as mine. Perhaps that would account for his surly behaviour.

'What was it like on your planet, Wolf?' I asked him.

'Not much to write home about,' was his reply.

'A bit like mine then,' I said, jokingly. 'Just me and Fiver sitting on a rock!'

'A bit like that,' Wolf replied.

'But, poor Lightning,' said Banana, touching my arm and causing me to flinch slightly. 'He had no one. Surely you had friends and family, Wolf?'

I looked down at Banana's hand. Although my initial reaction was to flinch, I was amazed to have someone so close to me. I felt happy but sad at the same time. Happy that I had a friend. Sad to think that until now I'd never known what having a friend could feel like. Sad to think that my parents had drifted off into space when they'd been ejected from our little craft.

'Not really,' was all Wolf would say.

I suddenly felt cross with Wolf for being so cagey. Surely his past wasn't as lonely as mine? Surely, he should be feeling sorry for me and not the other way around? But that was all we could get from him that day. Wolf growled between noisy mouthfuls of food and made sure his hair was always covering his eyes.

There were ten grades of classes, all on a rota for the two simulations rooms, and this meant that our crew only got a room twice a week. And because there were nine of us in our crew – ten if you included Fiver – we didn't get long to practise our individual powers.

The special effects were pretty basic. There was a giant screen at the back of the room and the lights would dim when the projector started up. Box-shaped spaceships would chug across from left to right, and from the bottom of the screen crocodile mouths popped up, snapping open and shut. Sometimes, they'd mix it up. Send the spaceships from the bottom and the crocodile heads from the left. And occasionally the professor would programme other creatures. Pink birds flying upside-down. Yellow smiling faces with black crosses for eyes. Piles of ammunition, guns, a rocket launcher.

The graphics were boxy and crude, but at least the screen was interactive. Still, it was nothing like the virtual reality simulation rooms you have now. No, it was very much two-dimensional, but the professor could programme the graphics on the screen to respond to each of our superpowers.

For most of us, that was straightforward enough. The professor could make the objects respond to my electricity, to Lava's lava, to Banana's vines or roots, to Obsidian's strength, to Laser's eyes, to Freeze's ice, to Wolf's claws, even.

At that point, the professor was still intent on All Powers becoming Potion. 'For each enemy who appears on the screen,' the professor told her, 'I will decide their superpower. You can then concoct a potion from plants to counter-attack their power and send it flying in a capsule towards the screen.'

Sometimes this seemed to work. All Powers would mix brightly coloured liquids in a bowl and shoot the potion over in a capsule, locking the jaws of crocodiles, causing the pink birds to fly the right way up, making guns shoot their own ammunition and spaceships return to their mother planet.

But sometimes All Powers couldn't resist the urge to use other powers. Sometimes lightning would shoot from her hands and fire down a spaceship. Lava would fire from her mouth and burn the jaws of a crocodile. Ice would travel down the length of her arms and shatter those yellow smiling faces.

Every time this happened, which was at least once a session, the professor would be patient with her, just like she was with all of us. 'Keep concentrating,' she'd tell her, 'and your other powers will fade and die out. It's just a matter of time, Potion.'

As I said, All Powers wasn't the only one who struggled in those early days in the simulation room. I know it sounds unthinkable, but I'd miss more of the objects than I'd hit. My score at the end of the session would regularly be lower than all of my superhero friends. But the professor's belief in us all, allied with Fiver's amazing ability to cheer us all up when we thought we were hopeless, meant that as the weeks passed, our scores got higher and it was anyone's guess which one of us would come second on the leader board that day.

We could only aspire as high as second place because of Tele. He was the only one that the simulation room didn't really challenge. Every day, even on a bad day, Tele's name would be top of the leader board. And, being Tele, he'd make sure he reminded us of this. 'When are you guys going to get your acts together?' Or, 'Don't any of you like the taste of victory?' Or, 'Since when has losing become so fashionable?'

I suppose from the start we accepted that showing-off was part of who Tele was. He'd always been a law unto himself. Flitting here and there at will. Teasing us. Trying to be as arrogantly unpredictable as possible. Perhaps we would have confronted him earlier if he hadn't been so charming about it. Told him that the only reason he was always top of the leader board was because the simulation just wasn't appropriate for his superpower. And I suppose, with the benefit of hindsight, that might have stopped him from making the decision that was to change his life for ever.

But, instead, we said nothing. Just laughed along with him. As the objects came across the screen, Tele would dodge them, using his power to disappear and reappear somewhere safe. It was just too easy. And, even though the professor would do her best to speed up the flying objects, to change their direction and their trajectory, Tele always disappeared before they reached him.

'La-la-la-la losers!' he'd shout at us, holding up his fingers in an L shape then his hand to high five us, taking it away before we made contact with him.

Sometimes this would amuse us. Other times it would annoy us. Especially Obsidian, who would pound his great fist on the floor, sending shock waves through the room.

At these moments it was Freeze who always stuck up for Tele. 'He's only joking with us,' Freeze would say.

But once the professor started taking us to the gym for some one-on-one combat, things became a lot less comfortable for Tele.

CHAPTER 10

WOLF SMILES

But, before I tell you about that, I need tell you more about Wolf. About how Wolf and I become close. About how we became best friends. My fourth ever friend after Fiver, Freeze and Banana.

It was my second night in the dorm. We were all in bed, tired after another day of thinking about our powers and how they might be used against our enemies. I assumed I'd be able to go straight to sleep. The mattress was still a novelty and Fiver was curled up snugly at my feet. I closed my eyes and waited for sleep to come, but memories came instead. Memories of me and Fiver playing around on the rocks. Me and Fiver running up the insides of craters. Me and Fiver reading *The War of the Worlds*. And then the memory of seeing my moon from far away on the spaceship after I'd been picked up by the scouts and realising how small and insignificant it was. And I felt sad. I remembered that my name was Mark. That I was Mark and not Lightning. That I couldn't remember having parents. That they had most probably died in the crash that had taken me and Fiver to the moon. And that my home was that small lonely moon and not this school.

Eventually I gave up on sleep. I opened my eyes to find Wolf staring down at me from his top bunk. I don't know how to explain what happened next. It was dark. Pitch black. And Wolf's eyes were black. Jet black. But, somehow, they seemed softer than they did in the daytime. Somehow, they seemed full of understanding. As if Wolf were having similar thoughts about his home planet. As if he was feeling sad too.

Without wanting to wake Fiver, I slipped out of my bed and walked over to Wolf's bunk. Our eyes were locked together, as if we were reading each other, trying to understand who each other was and, in doing so, trying to understand who we ourselves were.

It was Wolf who broke the silence. 'It's hard, isn't it?' he whispered gruffly.

I thought about saying *What is?* But that wouldn't have been fair because I knew exactly what he meant.

I nodded.

'I want to make friends,' Wolf continued, 'but I feel so different from everyone else.'

'Not *everyone*,' I replied.

'They think that I'm not one of them because I have animal powers.'

I remembered what the professor had said in our first lesson. 'That was just Obsidian. He just thinks he's so far advanced he knows everything.'

Wolf smiled and I could see the whites of his teeth. His canines were longer and sharper, more wolf-like, at night than in the day, and I noticed small black hairs surrounding his mouth now, too.

He suddenly seemed conscious of me staring and turned away before saying, 'Thanks, Mark.'

I was about to correct him, to say I was Lightning, but then I realised he'd said my real name deliberately. That it was his way of connecting with me. That we were friends now. And it meant that, despite everything that was to happen later, for my part we always would be.

The next day things seemed pretty much the same between us, but at the same time they were slightly different. OK,

Wolf didn't respond to Banana or me in the canteen, but neither did he growl, or glower, or completely avoid eye contact. In lessons, he sat to the right of me and once or twice, when I looked over at him, he held my gaze for a while, before looking away.

And then, a week or so later, there was another breakthrough!

The professor had taken us all down to the gym for a combat session. Tele had just experienced his first taste of defeat against Laser. As with all of us, the professor had made the two of them stand ten metres apart before blowing her whistle to let the battle commence. We had to wear red protective suits that were really heavy and slowed us down a bit. Every time the professor blew her whistle, Laser singed Tele's suit with his eyes before he could even think about disappearing.

Tele wasn't a good loser. 'Beginner's luck,' he told Laser after his first victory. Then, 'You looked before she whistled!' after his second victory. 'You cheated!' after finishing him off, three - nil. Freeze walked over to his friend to commiserate with him.

That day I was up against Wolf. As I knew we'd have one-on-one combat, I'd already planned what I'd do if I was paired against him. The key thing with Wolf, I knew, was to keep him away from you. In combat mode I'd seen him get down on his hands and knees and take on the stance of a wolf. Low to the ground, he'd move about swiftly, avoiding attacks that were thrown at him. Sometimes he'd pounce on his opponent, pinning them down, baring his teeth even. But, more often than not, he'd seem reluctant to do this. Preferring to give his opponent a chance. Not wanting to hurt them.

My plan that day wasn't particularly well thought through.

I guess I thought that because we now had a connection, because we were friends, he wouldn't pose too much of a threat to me. I'd keep Wolf away from me by overwhelming him before he even got close to the ground. Yes, I'd just blow him away! Use all of my electricity in one go. Then we'd laugh about it and it would bring us closer together than before.

What happened was quite different though. Sure enough, to the amusement of my fellow superheroes, I did shoot electricity all over the gym. It was a mighty, uncontrolled lightning storm, cracking against the walls and the ceiling, illuminating the gym bright white. Wolf just lowered himself to the ground, ducking below the storm with ease, even with his suit on, waiting for my power to falter and then stop. Once the tingling feeling had left my fingertips, I watched with a mixture of fear and disappointment as Wolf rose on his haunches and slowly stalked towards me. I knew that without any electricity it was pointless to try to put up a fight. But, as Wolf got close to me – close enough for me to smell his breath – I caught a glimpse of his long white canines and a flash of red in his eyes, which made me think that he might hurt me after all.

I stepped back from him and in that movement it was over. Wolf's canines were shorter and less pointy and back inside his mouth. His jet black eyes had softened, just like they had done that night.

Wolf stepped towards me again and I made myself stand still this time.

Placing his mouth against my ear, he whispered, 'Don't be in such a rush next time, Mark.'

'Good advice,' I whispered back.

As he moved away, he held my gaze with his jet black eyes. And then it happened. Wolf smiled.

DARK PLANET

After that, we were friends. We didn't say anything about being friends, of course. That wasn't Wolf's style. And there were still times in the canteen when Wolf preferred to remain silent instead of talking to me or Banana.

Some of the others had begun to try to make friends with him too. All Powers seemed particularly interested in Wolf. 'You're going to be a key member of our crew,' she'd tell him. 'I just know you are.'

The only ones who didn't seem to make an effort were Obsidian and Lava. Perhaps it was that they didn't want to bother when they could see that Wolf would give so little back in return. But perhaps it was also to do with their prejudice – their dislike of Wolf for his animalistic superpower.

With Wolf and me, the lack of words wasn't a problem, however. There was this feeling between us. A sense we shared about not feeling quite at home here at the superhero school. A sense of, *we don't belong here. This is not who we are*.

By this time, the professor had started to tell our crew more about Dark Planet. 'You need to understand your enemy in order to defeat them,' became the professor's favourite saying.

'Why did our war with Dark Planet begin in the first place?' the professor asked us. To my surprise, I realised that not only did I not know the answer to this most basic of basic questions, but neither did any of my superhero friends.

'Well,' the professor sighed, dismayed by our clear lack of historical knowledge, 'you need to go back almost forty years, to before the Intergalactic Alliance was formed. Indeed, the reason the Alliance formed in the first place was because of Dark Planet.'

I glanced over at Banana and we both raised our eyebrows in surprise. But, I thought in my own defence, I didn't have the opportunity for too many history lessons alone on the moon!

'Crocodile would have been young then,' the professor continued. 'Just out of school himself. Young and full of big ideas. Discovering he had the power to metamorphosise his mouth into the long, snapping mouth of a crocodile, he used his power to force the people of his own planet to work for him. Now, like all planets, most of the people have very limited powers, but some are stronger and, as far as we know, some of the people of Dark Planet have powers similar to our own superheroes. Some can make potions. Others can shoot lasers. Soar high in the sky like birds.'

'Some can bite like a wolf,' said Obsidian.

I looked over at Wolf. He was hunched over his desk, his hair covering his eyes.

'That may be the case,' replied the professor tersely, 'but that is not my point here. My point is that Crocodile discovered that, with just one bite, he could take their powers for his own, leaving the people feeling vulnerable and with a sense of loss. Without their powers they no longer knew who they were. Their only option was to work for him.

'But, as with most dictators, Crocodile's big ideas did not stop there. Not satisfied with having destroyed the collective will of his own people, Crocodile began using the flying powers he'd taken to explore the galaxy. Dark Planet had always been technologically behind and they didn't have spaceships back then. The power of flight enabled Crocodile to look for other planets and other powers he could steal and call his own. It didn't take him long to discover your planet, Lava and Obsidian, and to start taking the powers away from its inhabitants. But, unlike the people of Dark Planet, the people of Red Planet weren't so quick to submit to Crocodile's brutal ways. Instead, they fought back like warriors, hurling lumps of rock and lava from the Red Planet's fiery surface.

'Red Planet had already made contact with the other planets in our galaxy to warn them about Crocodile. Red Planet made three proposals. First of all, they suggested we form an alliance of planets to share information and protect each other from evil, as they suspected this wouldn't be the last they'd see of Crocodile. Secondly, they suggested that the Alliance set up a superhero school to nurture those with the strongest powers to fight Crocodile and the people of Dark Planet. And, thirdly, they would recruit those with the strongest powers to surround Dark Planet in a ring of fire to trap Crocodile and his people. There have been times when the ring of fire has been breached and that's where we come in. The school trains the superheroes of the future who will defeat Crocodile.'

When she'd finished her story, the professor asked us if we had any questions.

Before I came to the school, I had no sense of history beyond the moon. The history of the galaxy as told by the professor was the only real history I now knew. It made perfect sense to me and, I have to say, I felt happier for it. As if I now had a real purpose. A reason to be here, to be part of this crew, to willingly give up being Mark and become Lightning.

I now realise that I just didn't know any better than to question the Alliance's version of history.

The only person to speak was Wolf. 'How do you know all that's true, Professor?' he asked, scowling slightly before turning his scowl into a smile that revealed his canine teeth.

The professor seemed taken aback by this and, for the first time since we'd known her, unsure of what to say. After a moment, she composed herself and replied, 'That's a fair question, Wolf. The history is written in many books and the books are written from witness statements, which are kept – correct me if I'm wrong, Lava and Obsidian – in the library on Red Planet.'

Wolf directed his jet black eyes to Lava and Obsidian.

Lava was effusive in her support of what the professor had said. 'That's right, Professor, we learnt all about it at school.'

If that were the case, I wondered why they had been unable to answer the professor's question at the start of the lesson.

'Why don't you believe the professor, Wolf?' Obsidian asked accusingly. 'It's almost as if you don't want to help the Alliance defeat Dark Planet.'

Wolf looked intently at Lava before lowering his head and letting his dark hair cover his eyes.

It was All Powers who came to Wolf's rescue. 'That's not what Wolf's saying,' she insisted. 'He's just saying that it's important to look at the evidence before coming to conclusions about what happened and who did what.'

'Didn't sound that way to me,' Obsidian replied. 'Sounded to me like–'

'And we've heard quite enough from you, Obsidian,' the professor interrupted. 'If there's no more questions, we'll call it a day.'

ALL POWERS

After weeks of honing our individual skills, we moved to phase two. At first the group tasks were straightforward enough. The professor would give us a scenario in which our crew would be set upon by people from Dark Planet. We'd have to work out what powers they had and which of our collective powers would be best suited to destroying them.

'Remember, when this happens for real,' the professor would always say, 'you won't have the luxury of discussion time. Your collective response needs to become instinctive. You need to practise these drills until you all know instantly what each other is thinking and what each of you are going to do.'

At first there was a lot of debate about the primary line of attack. Was the best way to eliminate a shark-like enemy to electrocute them or to freeze them? Should you laser an enemy who had bird powers or capture them in vines instead? And, when a group of giant enemies were descending upon you like a herd of rhinoceroses, was it best to stand up against them like a wall of rock, or to slow them down and burn them with a wave of lava?

These debates could easily have led to fallings out within the group, but there were two main reasons they didn't. First of all, there was Fiver. My dog, my only friend on the moon, could calm any one of us just by rubbing himself against our legs and looking up at us with his big docile eyes. As soon as Obsidian or Laser, or whoever was feeling left out, bent to stroke Fiver they seemed instantly placated, calm and able to accept someone else's point of view.

The second reason our crew was so good together was All Powers. We were still calling her Potion at the time, but it was becoming clear to all of us, the professor included, that her powers couldn't be constricted to just making potions. I am not exaggerating; she could do anything! And because she could do anything, she possessed a skill that was undoubtedly more formidable than all of the powers put together. She had the skill of diplomacy. She knew what each power felt like; what it felt like to be each of us possessing our powers. She could, therefore, understand everyone's opinion and help the crew to make a decision that we would ultimately agree was the best one.

'That's a great point, Freeze,' she would say enthusiastically. 'You could definitely create a sheet of ice, making it difficult for the lion enemy to stand. But it might be worth letting Tele act as bait first to lure the enemies to the place where you can lay the ice. He can disappear to safety and you can cause chaos before Wolf finishes them off.'

All Powers always spoke positively about Wolf, trying to lift his spirits and make him feel part of the crew. Lava and Obsidian didn't always like this, but when they challenged her she'd always find a calm resolution.

'Why Wolf?' Obsidian had asked on one occasion. 'Surely it would be better for me to crush them with my little finger. Wolf wouldn't be that reliable in battle.'

'I'd say that Wolf would be the most reliable in battle,' All Powers responded. 'He's fearless and that means he wouldn't think twice. But, of course, you will have your part to play too, Obsidian.'

As we worked our way through hundreds of different scenarios, the professor would observe us, writing down notes on a small pad, feeding back her thoughts at the end of the session.

After one discussion where All Powers had been particularly adept in gaining group consensus about how to deal with a plague of enemies with bat-like qualities, the professor looked directly at her and said, jokingly, 'Perhaps I was wrong in calling you Potion. Clearly your powers are in diplomacy. We should call you Diplomacy!'

I think she thought she'd laugh at this, but All Power's face turned serious and, when she spoke, she spoke carefully and deliberately. 'I'm sorry, Professor, I don't mean to be disrespectful to you, but I just don't feel that Potion is who I am. Potion is just a small part of me. As a superhero, I am so many other things. I am Lightning, I am Freeze, I am Laser, Wolf, even Tele – without the arrogance, that is!'

'You'd never be as good as me!' smiled Tele.

The professor looked sad. 'But how can you possibly practise all of your powers? And, without practising all of your powers, how can you possibly help the crew?'

Fiver scampered over to the professor, brushing against her leg. All Powers smiled and said, 'That's all I do, Professor, every moment, awake or asleep. In my head I'm constantly practising all my powers. I know that none of the individual powers will ever be quite as strong as if I just had one power. I understand that. But I think I can still make them all strong. And I feel like if I don't, if I just keep them all in my head, one day I'm going to burst!'

The professor bent down to stroke Fiver. That was always a good sign.

'Besides, being All Powers gives the crew ultimate flexibility. It means I can be whoever the they need me to be at any given moment.'

To be fair to the professor, she could have put her foot

down and said no, or mixed up a potion to make All Powers believe she was Potion and no one else. But instead she just smiled. 'Now I really do believe I should be calling you Diplomacy. But diplomacy is obviously the power you gain from understanding all of the other superpowers.' Picking up Fiver, the professor smiled. 'All Powers it is then.'

HOW TO DEFEAT CROCODILE

The professor's agreement came with one condition – that All Powers joined one of the other grades to allow her more time practising her powers in a simulation room. This may have been good for All Powers, but it was not so good for the crew. The professor kept giving us different enemies to defeat in different situations, but without All Powers there to act as our diplomat it took a lot longer for us to come to an agreement.

Our loss was felt particularly strongly by Wolf. Without All Powers there to sing his virtues, Obsidian and Lava found it easier to exclude him.

Sometimes their tactics were subtle. The professor would ask us to talk through a simulation as a group in order to decide how best to deal with the enemy that was being presented to us. Lava would take control in these situations, saying what she thought and then directing questions at the rest of us, always starting with her best friend.

'What's your take on this Obsidian? ... Great point... How about you Laser? ... And you Banana? ... Freeze? ... Lightning? ... Tele?'

She would never once ask Wolf what he thought.

Sometimes their tactics were painfully obvious. From time to time, Wolf would offer his opinion only for Obsidian or Lava, or sometimes both, to laugh at him dismissively.

'In this situation we could ask All Powers what we should do,' Wolf suggested.

'Hah!' laughed Obsidian. 'That's the spirit. Let someone else do all the work!'

Or he'd say, 'I could use their scent to track them down.'

'You'd probably end up taking us straight to the toilet,' Lava retorted.

I still blame myself, of course I do. I should have stuck up for him. Banana tried, and when All Powers returned *she* definitely did, but for some reason Lava and Obsidian made a formidable duo and it was easier for the rest of us to either laugh along with them or at least remain silent rather than go against them.

Then one day the professor asked us to imagine that we had come face-to-face with Crocodile. At the mere mention of his name, all of us, myself included, became hot-headed. All of us were thinking of our own powers and how we could use them to defeat Crocodile. How we could gain glory.

'First of all, I'll freeze his jaw shut.' That was Freeze.

'First of all, *I'll* clamp his jaw shut.' Obsidian.

'*I'll* burn him.' Lava.

'No, *I'll* laser him.' Laser.

'Snare his jaws.' Banana.

'We should lure him to us.' Tele.

'Why not just get on with it – fry him!' I'm ashamed to say that was me.

Poor Fiver. He didn't know which one of us to run to!

The only superhero to hold back was Wolf.

'What do *you* think, Wolf?' the professor asked eventually, frustrated no doubt by the selfishness the rest of us were displaying. By this stage in our training it was unusual for the professor to intervene in this way, but without All Powers there to help us she'd clearly had enough of our bickering.

For a while, Wolf didn't respond. He hung his head

slightly, letting his hair cover his eyes, as he always did when he wanted to hide away.

Given Wolf's silence, I expected the professor to keep talking. To save Wolf from having to speak. But the professor held her ground and said nothing.

Eventually Wolf lifted his head and pulled his hair from his face. 'I'm thinking, what if you are all wrong about Crocodile? I'm thinking, what if Crocodile is not really so evil after all?'

Banana reached for my hand. I'd learnt not to flinch when she did this and I took her hand gratefully as we exchanged an awkward glance. Just like the other day when All Powers had insisted she was All Powers and not Potion, the professor seemed to not know what to say.

Crocodile not evil after all? Crocodile not the person we'd all been told about? The whole of intergalactic history rewritten in such an extraordinary way?

The very idea was unthinkable to all of us. We just couldn't comprehend it.

Of course, Obsidian and Lava didn't hold back.

'Traitor!' said Obsidian.

'Dark Planet lover!' said Lava.

'Enough!' snapped the professor, her uncertainty suddenly replaced by seriousness. She dismissed the rest of us and said, 'Wolf, I'd like a quick word before you join the others in the canteen please.'

CHAPTER 14
THE GOLDEN DISK

I don't know what the professor said to Wolf. Dinner in the canteen was awkward to say the least. Lava and Obsidian were muttering away to themselves and, when Wolf joined us, I could feel them staring at him and I didn't know what to say.

Banana smiled at him and Wolf did that thing where he let his hair fall over his eyes.

'It's OK, Wolf,' I said, as quietly as I could.

But Wolf just shook his head. 'It's not OK, Mark,' he whispered gruffly.

I could sense Banana looking at me, aware Wolf had used my real name.

By this time, All Powers had come to our end of the table. She crouched down next to Wolf. 'Nothing's as simple as people make out, Wolf,' she began. 'Good and evil exists, but it exists everywhere.'

I wasn't sure what she meant by this. I've always been a little slow to cotton on. But Wolf seemed to take heart in her words and lifted his head to smile at her.

'It just feels like the history they're telling us is so simple, so one-sided,' Wolf said.

Lying in bed that night, their words ran through my mind and I tried to imagine what Dark Planet was really like. What the people were like. What Crocodile was like too. I couldn't sleep. The history the professor had told us had given me an identity and a purpose. I was Lightning, a superhero trained to protect the Alliance from Dark Planet. But what if the Alliance didn't really need protecting? What if the people of Dark Planet, Crocodile included, weren't really bad? Who was I then? A boy alone on a rock with a five-legged dog and book which belongs to Mark?

I looked over to Wolf's bunk, hoping to find him awake too, but for once his eyes were shut. This was unusual. I'd never known Wolf to go to sleep before me. So unusual, in fact, that I got out of my bunk to stand up and watch him sleeping. His breathing was steady and his face was peaceful, but now completely covered in short black bristly hairs.

I must have slept because the next morning I woke up to find the others talking.

'Who did that?' Lava was demanding, pointing at the door.

'Can only have been Wolf,' Obsidian said matter-of-factly.

I sat up to see the length of the door had been scarred by ten deep scratch marks. Wolf was sitting up in bed too. I thought about the previous night and how Wolf had been the first to sleep and how his face had become covered with bristly black hairs.

I expected Wolf to defend himself but instead he just looked sad and said, 'I'm sorry.'

'Tell that to the door,' replied Tele.

Not long after the Crocodile incident the professor came into class smiling at us and holding aloft a shiny gold disc.

'Do any of you know what this is?' she asked us, flipping the disc over and showing that it had marks on both sides – squares, rectangles, a star shape and some zigzags engraved on the disc's hard surface. The professor brought the disc closer to us and we could see there was a small hole in the centre and faint circular grooves going all the way round.

'No? Well, it's a disc, what some people call a record – a very old-fashioned way of playing music,' the professor explained. 'It was found yesterday orbiting the school just outside the security circle. One of the professors played it in the staffroom last night and it's full of these strange noises and different voices. No one could make head nor tail of it and I asked if I could share it with my crew. With you.'

I turned to Banana, who was already smiling, excited by the prospect of being given a real challenge to discuss.

The professor raised her eyebrows. 'Now, some of the professors said you weren't ready to tackle your first real-life problem, but I begged to differ. I said I had never worked with a crew who possessed such great individual and collective powers. That this crew might still be inexperienced when it comes to protecting the galaxy, but that the only way to change that is to be given responsibility. And besides,' the professor laughed, 'sitting in a classroom and trying to work out what a golden disc means is hardly a dangerous first mission, now, is it?'

If only the professor could have known how she'd have to eat those words!

She went into one of the store cupboards and wheeled out a box with a lever on top. She put the disc on the box, waited for it to start spinning, then placed the lever on the disc. We all listened carefully. When the disc had finished playing she turned it over and played the other side.

Of course, most of you here today will be familiar with the golden disc. Your parents will have played you the sounds of the people, the birds, the animals, the wind, the rain and sea, the musical instruments, the melodies and the harmonies.

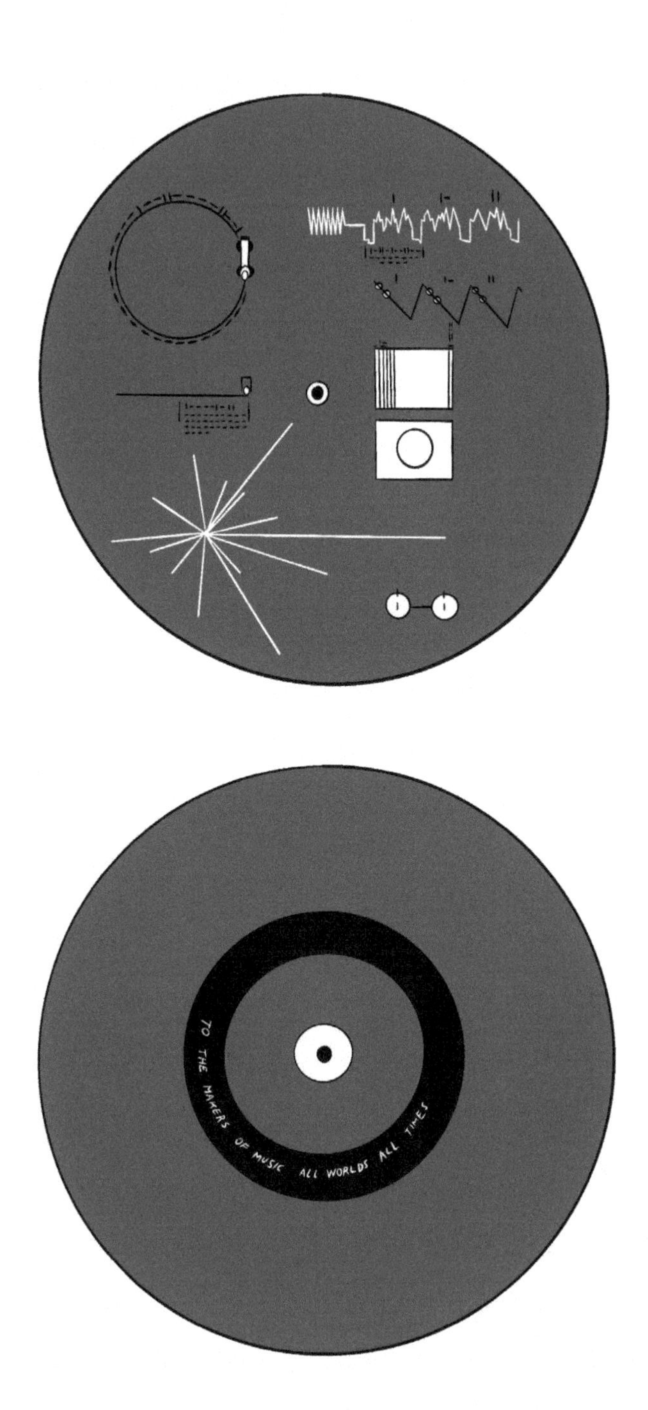
TO THE MAKERS OF MUSIC ALL WORLDS ALL TIMES

And you will all know what the sounds are, where they were recorded and how they were made. But for us, sitting there in Professor Banks's classroom, listening to the sounds for the first time, it was almost impossible to work out what they might mean.

We had lots of ideas though.

'I know that sound,' said Lava. 'It's the sound of a distant volcano erupting.'

'And I know that one,' said Banana. 'It's the sound of someone hunting. Listen to the great whooshing noise it makes.'

'That cracking sound,' offered Freeze, 'could be an ice-cap melting?'

'And those voices,' said All Powers, 'they are lots of different people, all speaking in different languages.'

We went on like that, sharing our ideas, asking the professor to play the bit where there was music again. At one point, Banana stood up and grabbed hold of me (I didn't flinch) and we did this silly dance together. I realised I'd never really danced before and I felt disappointed when she stopped.

'I knew you were ready for this,' said the professor after she'd played the golden disc for the fifth time and we'd had a go at identifying each and every sound. 'But, I suppose the question is, what does it all mean? Who sent the golden disc and what was their motivation for sending it?'

I tried to think of answers to the professor's questions but, like the rest of the crew, I drew a blank. As I became more frustrated with myself I could feel the tingle of electricity building up in my fingertips.

It was Wolf who broke the silence. 'I recognise the languages, Professor, from when I was in school. We had a lesson about some of the distant planets in the galaxy and we learnt about their languages. One of the planets was called Earth. These, I think, are the voices of children from Planet Earth.'

The professor smiled at Wolf. 'Very good,' she said. 'I was thinking that too.'

'And the sounds of their planet and the people on the planet,' Wolf continued uncertainly, 'could be telling us that Earth is in trouble. That their way of life is under threat. That they are experiencing great changes. Dangerous changes. And that they need our help.'

Looking back now, like the rest of you, I can see that Wolf's theory wasn't wholly supported by what was actually on the golden disc. However, Wolf's theory became instantly popular with our crew because it gave us a purpose. Surprisingly, it was Obsidian and Lava who were most pleased with it.

'We must go to Planet Earth!' bellowed Obsidian.

'We can save them!' chimed Lava.

And, within the space of a few minutes, most of the crew were talking enthusiastically about what would become our first mission. To go to Planet Earth. To save Planet Earth.

A MESSAGE FROM PLANET EARTH

The professor, however, was having none of it. I have to admit this was a relief to me. 'It's a good theory,' she told Wolf, 'but it's just a theory.'

Strangely, Wolf said that he agreed. 'I'm pretty sure it's from Planet Earth, Professor, but they could be saying something quite different.'

'Like what?' said Banana quickly. She was already imagining us all on the spaceship and she didn't want the professor talking us out of it. 'I mean why would Planet Earth send a message on a disc if they didn't want our help?'

'To say hello?' This was Wolf again. 'To communicate with planets in other galaxies?'

'No,' said Freeze, also evidently imagining us all taking off on our first mission. 'Your other theory was the better theory, Wolf. You wouldn't go to the trouble of making a disc like that if you just wanted to say hello.'

The rest of us nodded in agreement. Obsidian banged his fist on his desk and Lava said, 'It's the best contribution Wolf's ever made.'

'Let's just think through Wolf's second theory,' said All Powers, her power of diplomacy coming to the fore. 'It is possible that Planet Earth did just want to make contact with beings on other planets, isn't it, Professor? I mean, am I right in thinking that not much is known about the people on Planet Earth?'

'That's correct, All Powers,' said the professor. 'Earth is

a long way away from us, about a hundred galaxies to be precise, and this means that whilst lots of astronauts have taken photos of what they sometimes call Blue Planet, only two spaceships have ever landed there. The first mission never returned and the second, more recent, mission reported finding very little of interest. Just water, mainly water, and a book called an encyclopedia. This has been translated for our school children to learn about. The idea of the missions had been to see if the people of Earth would become part of our Intergalactic Alliance,' the professor laughed. 'The fish, apparently, weren't that responsive to our invitation!'

'Maybe they didn't look hard enough,' said Laser.

'Yes, maybe there are people there,' said Banana.

Professor Banks looked unconvinced. 'It's possible,' she said, 'but unlikely. Wolf, this was your theory. What do you think?'

Even though Wolf and I had become friends, it didn't mean he always looked happy in my company. Whatever was going on, Wolf always had the same surly expression. As if he wasn't particularly enjoying what was happening, even if he actually was. But I looked over at my friend and was surprised at what I saw. He was smiling awkwardly. As if he were uncertain about what he was going to say. As if he were slightly afraid.

'I think, Professor,' Wolf began, 'that it's possible there are still some people on Planet Earth. Maybe this disc was sent by them a long time ago and has taken an even longer time to reach us. Maybe now the people are no more. But, I suppose, I would say what's the harm in the school sending an experienced group of superheroes, professors maybe, to Earth to find out? If there are people still alive, we could help them; if there aren't, the professors can do some fishing and then come home.'

A great banging noise came from Obsidian's desk, but this time the noise was of disagreement and not approval. '*We* should go to Planet Earth,' Obsidian shouted defiantly, his voice echoing through the superhero school.

'Completely out of the question,' the professor quickly replied. 'I'll take it to the professors. Some of them, or perhaps some more experienced superheroes, may go, but to send first graders all the way to Earth – why, that would be ridiculous!'

With the exception of Wolf and I, the others continued with their objections. Aside from the moon, the school was the only home I knew and I had no great desire to leave it.

CHAPTER 16 THE RENEGADE MISSION

In the canteen, however, the others hatched a plan to form a renegade mission to travel to Planet Earth.

Lava was the ringleader, backed at every moment by Obsidian. 'We'll go anyway,' she announced the next morning over breakfast.

'We will,' chimed Obsidian, as if no other outcome were possible.

I could sense Banana getting excited beside me. 'But how?' she asked them.

Lava and Obsidian looked blankly at each other before turning to All Powers.

All Powers smiled. 'This would be sneaky of us,' she said. 'But we could ask the professor to continue to train us as *if* we were preparing for a mission to Planet Earth. We'll make it clear we have no intention of going, that we understand we won't be going. But, when we've got enough knowledge and skills, we'll set off under the cover of darkness.'

All Powers being so sneaky and calculated surprised and alarmed me. But I supposed that as All Powers her powers would include ones of a more sinister nature. She even managed to justify the planned deception when Wolf challenged her.

'We can't abuse the professor's trust in that way,' said Wolf.

'I know what you are saying,' All Powers agreed, 'but you have to remember why we're doing this. It's not for us,' she paused and glanced meaningfully over at Obsidian and Lava. 'It's for the people of Planet Earth. They need us.'

Once the plan was hatched it became almost impossible to stop them. Wolf and I were the only ones who weren't keen on going and we talked about it in the canteen queue.

'It's the professor I feel sorry for,' Wolf said. 'She's such a trusting, reasonable person that when Lava suggested we should pretend to train for a mission to Earth, she didn't for one second question us.'

'Agreed. But, if I'm really honest with you, Wolf, the main reason I don't want to go to Earth is that I'm happy here with you and Banana and everyone in the school. Why would I want to leave when it feels like I've finally found a home?'

Wolf looked into my eyes and I felt that connection again. 'We'll do what we can to stop them,' he promised.

'But we won't tell,' I added. 'I can't bear the thought of betraying any of them.'

'I might just tell on Lava and Obsidian,' Wolf laughed, flashing a smile at me.

We spent the next few days preparing for our 'mission'. 'The journey would be the toughest part,' the poor professor explained earnestly. 'Nine of you on a spaceship travelling through a hundred galaxies. It'd take you about a month to get there and, believe me, that month would feel like a lifetime. You'd be bored, restless and claustrophobic. You'd have nowhere to practise your superpowers.' The professor bent down to stroke Fiver who was nestling against her legs. 'But you'd have Fiver, of course, to help you.'

We spent days in the spaceship which was docked in the school reception. The professor asked us to imagine moons and planets rushing past us, because that's what it would feel like once we'd set off. We took it in turns at the control deck, the professor talking us through which buttons to press. One time, when I was in the driving seat, I got the tingling sensation in my hands so badly that I couldn't help but shake them. A sheet of lightning burnt a small hole in the floor.

'Doing that when you're in space would be catastrophic,' the professor told me. 'You'd need to keep your lightning in, Lightning. Or, if you have to, use it to recharge some of the batteries onboard the ship.'

The idea of the batteries was a good one and made me feel better about the journey. It also prompted the other superheroes to think about how they could use their powers on the spaceship.

'I'll throw sticks for Fiver so that he can fetch them,' said Banana.

'I'll drip my lava onto Obsidian so that he can grow even bigger,' said Lava.

'Before it sets, I'll laser some of the lava you put onto Obsidian so that he doesn't grow too big,' said Laser.

'Before you laser it, I'll freeze the lava so that it doesn't cause the ship, or the rest of us, to burn,' said Freeze.

'I'll use my power of diplomacy to work with Fiver and ensure we're all still friends by the time we get to Planet Earth,' said All Powers.

'And you, Tele? What would you do?' the professor asked.

'I'd just avoid the spaceship part altogether, Prof,' said Tele casually.

'You would?' said the Professor, sounding doubtful.

'Yep, I'd teleport there!' Tele replied.

The professor started laughing. 'You'd teleport across a hundred galaxies? It's one thing teleporting to other side of a simulation room, but quite another to teleport from here to Planet Earth!'

'I've got the skills, Prof,' insisted Tele.

'Well,' said the professor, adopting her serious voice. 'Whether or not you've got the skills is irrelevant. If you were going on a mission to Planet Earth, which thankfully you are not, you wouldn't be doing it like that, Tele. It'd be too much of a risk. You'd have to make do with teleporting yourself to the other side of the spaceship.' Before Tele could argue, the professor turned to Wolf. 'And, Wolf, what would you propose?'

'I become more like a wolf at night, but if I stay awake I can control my wolfish instincts,' Wolf said.

'You'd propose to stay awake for 30 days and nights?' the professor asked.

'Yes,' Wolf replied. 'It wouldn't be that hard. I've stayed awake most nights since I've been here. I don't need much sleep.'

I thought about the ten scratch marks on our bedroom door. I pictured Wolf in his bunk every night, the whites of his eyes wide and bright, staring down at me. And I understood for the first time that, despite our connection, he wasn't quite the same as me after all. It wasn't that he couldn't sleep because he didn't know who he was. Rather, he wouldn't let himself sleep because he *did* know who he was. And he was afraid of who he was. He was afraid of what he might do to us.

'I've been thinking, Professor,' Wolf said, looking at the rest of the crew. 'I was probably wrong about the disc. Maybe the people of Earth don't need our help. Maybe there aren't any people left on Earth to need our help. Maybe the disc was sent when they were still alive. Maybe we shouldn't be pretending to go there after all.'

The professor smiled at Wolf. 'That's a lot of maybes, Wolf. And it's common to feel anxious before a mission. Even a pretend mission. But try not to worry so much. I've spoken to the professors about your initial theory and they are in no rush to put a crew together. Like you, they think it's highly unlikely there are any people left on Earth.'

It's obvious now, but at the time none of us had any idea why Wolf really didn't want us to go to Planet Earth. None of us, myself included, realised just how conflicted Wolf was.

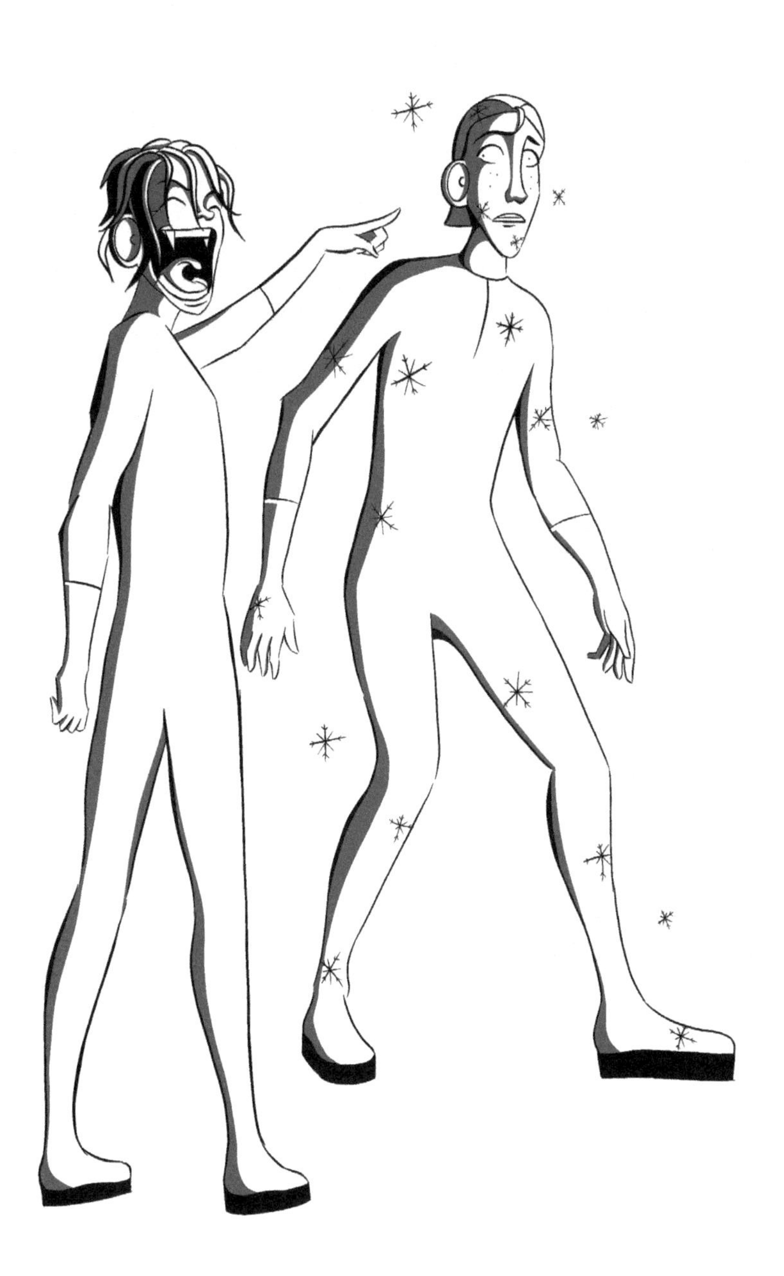

TAKE OFF

Then, one evening in the canteen, Lava said that it was time. 'The professor's finished our pretend training. We'll meet in reception at midnight.'

'What if one of the officers questions us?' I asked, really not wanting to leave.

Lava looked over at All Powers. 'We'll say it's just part of our training. That the professor has asked us to simulate a take-off.'

Wolf almost spat out his food. 'That'll never work,' he said.

But work it did. That evening the nine of us were standing in reception easily convincing the officer on duty that he should unlock the spaceship so that we could simulate our take-off.

I'd been counting on the officer refusing our request, but he just said, 'Right you are then,' and pressed the button which opened the spaceship.

I felt sick in my stomach at the thought of leaving and I could feel a trembling at the bottom of my legs. I didn't want to go but it wasn't *my* legs that were trembling. No, it was poor Fiver, cowering beside me, suddenly aware that things weren't quite right, that we were about to enter the spaceship.

Fiver and I weren't the only ones to feel overwhelmed. The others began to make their way on board, but as Freeze strode towards the spaceship he suddenly froze.

'Don't worry,' said All Powers. 'It's just nerves. It's

what they don't tell you in books and films about being a superhero. Superheroes get nervous too! Even when it's just a simulation flight.'

'But he's frozen himself to the spot,' Wolf said.

It was true. Freeze had turned his already cold body into a giant lump of ice.

'Maybe we should stay here,' continued Wolf. 'Maybe we should postpone the trip.'

'There have been too many maybes from you lately, Wolf,' said Lava. 'All Powers, what do you think we should do?'

All Powers was deep in thought. 'I think Laser should defrost him,' she said eventually.

Lava agreed. Laser lowered his lasers to their weakest setting before beginning the defrost processes, working upwards from the tips of Freeze's toes right up to the hairs on his head.

All of us were so engrossed by the spectacle of Freeze defrosting that we didn't notice what Tele was doing. It was only once Lava had welcomed Freeze back to life and congratulated All Powers on her calmness in decision making and Laser on the skilful control of his laser eyes in defrost-mode, that we noticed Tele was missing.

'Did anyone see him go?' All Powers asked us. 'Did anyone speak to him this morning or last night about his plans?'

None of us did but we all knew what had happened. Freeze, his best friend in the school, was the most upset. 'It's all my fault,' he said. 'If I hadn't frozen he would be here still.'

Banana put her arm around Freeze. 'That's not true,' she told him. 'He would have gone anyway. None of us could have stopped him. You know what he's like once he gets an idea in his head.'

'Do you think he'll make it?' Wolf asked Lava pointedly.

Lava said nothing, but she looked concerned.

'It's certainly possible,' said All Powers. 'If anyone can, Tele can!'

We weren't convinced, but Lava wouldn't let us dwell too much on Tele's decision and instead ushered us onto the spaceship.

As we stepped inside I thought I might actually be sick. I glanced at Wolf but he just looked at the floor. Lava had already taken the controls. Whether we liked it or not, we were on our way to Planet Earth.

CHAPTER 18
JOURNEY TO PLANET EARTH

In the back of my mind I was still hopeful that they wouldn't let us through the security circle. But it turned out the security circle was designed to stop things coming into the school rather than going out. As Lava slowed the spaceship down the jaws of the checkpoint open submissively. Lava unplugged the communication system, pre-empting an early morning call from the professor, and we were well and truly on our way.

I won't bore you with of all the details of our thirty-day journey to Planet Earth. But I'll give you some of the highlights, although there weren't many!

We spent a lot of our time speculating on whether Tele had made it. Whether or not we actually believed it, most of us said we thought he had, and that when we landed we would find him waiting. The thought of seeing his friend again really cheered Freeze up.

The one exception was Wolf.

'Why are you so negative, Wolf?' Banana asked brightly.

'Am I?' said Wolf, as if he didn't know what she was talking about.

'Yes, you are,' insisted Banana, still smiling. 'Ever since you decoded the golden disc, you've been negative about this whole trip.'

Wolf lowered his head, letting his brown hair cover his eyes.

'Maybe,' I began, deciding it was best to speak for my

friend, 'he's just being cautious. It is our first mission, after all, and it's a renegade mission as well. It would be easy for a mission like this to fail because of the over-confidence of the crew.'

'Maybe!' replied Banana.

I could sense that Wolf still wasn't going to respond himself, so I quickly changed the subject. To try and convince myself that the mission would be OK and that we'd be home at the school very soon, Banana and I began to imagine what it would be like on Planet Earth.

The funniest sight on that long trip was when Lava got rid of some of the lava that was building up inside of her.

'I'm ready,' she'd say to Obsidian. Wordlessly, Obsidian would come and sit beside his friend.

'Where do you want it today?' Lava would ask him.

Obsidian was always careful to choose a different part of his body. "I want to spread it out evenly. That will make me stronger all over' he explained.

Once they'd picked a spot, Lava would position herself so that she could slowly expel a gentle flow of lava from her mouth onto Obsidian. This was difficult because there was zero gravity so Obsidian would have to position himself carefully next to or even above Lava as she performed her outpouring. Here Freeze would take over. He'd isolate the burning red lava that was now clinging to Obsidian and freeze it slowly but surely with the ice-cold touch of his hands. Once frozen, Laser would get to work, using his eyes with great dexterity to burn and remove any lumps. After he'd finished and the lava had returned to room temperature, Obsidian would just look a little more muscular than he had before.

'Check out my new eight-pack!' he'd joke. Or, 'Look at

this for a double bicep!'

The metamorphosis of Obsidian from the strongest superhero ever to an even stronger strongest superhero ever was truly a sight to behold!

And to his credit, Fiver got used to being cooped up with eight superheroes for all that time. Banana was excellent with him. She was enthusiastic anyway – for me, her enthusiasm was always her real power. Seeing poor Fiver looking so sad, she directed her enthusiasm towards making him feel better.

It wasn't long before chasing sticks became Fiver's favourite sport. The first time they tried it went slightly wrong. The stick flew too fast and although Fiver caught it, it cut his gum. But Banana quickly adapted, softening her throw, making it difficult for Fiver but without hurting him.

Chasing a stick in a small spaceship, in zero gravity, proved to be great fun. Banana would lightly flick a stick and Fiver would watch it glide its way slowly across the cabin before launching himself off the floor with his hind legs, catching up with it, and firmly clamping it in his mouth.

The plan was that at night-time we'd take it in turn to control the spaceship, but this didn't last long.

'I prefer to drive at night,' Wolf told us. 'I don't want to sleep anyway,' he added. Remembering what he'd done to the door that night when he had slept, we didn't disagree with him.

Some nights, I'd stay awake and keep him company. I didn't sleep much myself on the spaceship. Being in space with no solid ground was exciting, but it was also quite unsettling. I worried about the professor disowning us when we returned. I watched the planets and stars go past us and I would have moments where I couldn't remember who I was or where I was from. I'd think about being Mark. Being on the moon with Fiver, exploring the craters, blasting the rock. Then I'd feel the weightlessness of being here on the spaceship, with these people who I didn't really know.

Sitting up at the front with Wolf helped. We didn't speak much – he wasn't a talker and nor was I having spent most of my life living by myself – but just being together helped me feel more certain about who I was.

When we did talk, we focused on how impossible it had been to stop this renegade mission. But how we hadn't wanted to be left behind if the rest of them were going.

'It wouldn't have been the same,' I said, imagining the two of us and Fiver in the empty classroom with the professor.

'And we would have had to tell her all about their plan,' Wolf replied.

'At least this way the professor might forgive us if we do actually save Planet Earth.'

'I wouldn't count on it,' said Wolf.

I didn't ask him whether he meant the professor forgiving us or saving Planet Earth.

One night I asked what he thought we'd find there.

Wolf didn't say anything for a while. Finally, he muttered, 'I hope we find some nice people we can help.'

'You *hope*?' I replied.

'Yes,' said Wolf, flashing the infra-red of his jet black eyes at me, digging his fingernails into his blue trousers. 'How can any of us know what we will really find there?'

I nodded my head until I could see his fingers relax. I knew when it was best not to push him any further.

'I guess we'll see,' I said.

And it wasn't long before we did see. In just a matter of days we were slowing down, gliding towards the Blue Planet.

CHAPTER 19
LANDING ON EARTH

The landing wasn't particularly heroic. We'd all agreed that Lava should be at the controls and as the blue of Blue Planet got ever closer to us. All Powers joined her up front to try to decide where we should land.

'We've got no choice,' I could hear All Powers saying. 'We're going to have to land on the water.'

To be fair to Lava, she managed to slow the spaceship down enough to ensure a smoothish landing and, crucially, was able to ensure that instead of diving into the water, our spaceship floated on top of it.

Freeze made his way straight to the door, no doubt keen to see if Tele was there. To his disappointment, there was only water.

We stood there for a while looking at the water. It was choppy and windy and there were small droplets of water in the air.

I turned to All Powers. 'What shall we do?' I asked her.

'This isn't the place,' she said. 'We need to find out where the people are. That way we can find Tele. He would have teleported to where the people are.'

'If there are actually any people here,' said Wolf. 'Perhaps we should just go home.'

Freeze turned on Wolf with his icy stare. 'We're not going anywhere without Tele,' he insisted. 'If you lot just want to stand around doing nothing then I'll go and find him myself.'

And, with that, Freeze directed the ice-cold power of his hands towards the great mass of water outside the spaceship.

'You can't freeze all of that,' insisted Wolf.

'Watch me!' said Freeze.

Of course, Wolf was right. It would have taken Freeze all of his life and all of his powers to freeze all of the water on Earth. They don't call it Blue Planet for nothing!

But to his credit, Freeze did manage to still the waves lapping at our spaceship and create a platform which we could all step out on.

He would have done more than this, of course. He would have done anything if he thought it would have helped his friend. But after a while, Banana put her arm around his cold body, for as long as she could anyway. Then All Powers said, 'I have an idea.'

CHAPTER 20
PEOPLE OF THE VOLCANO

All Power's idea, of course, was a good one.

'One of the powers that I've been practising is the power of mental communication, or telepathy.'

'You mean mind reading?' asked Wolf, sounding concerned.

All Powers laughed. 'Yes,' she said, 'but don't worry, Wolf. I won't be reading your mind. I would need all of my power for that! Anyway, I'm pretty sure that if we get back in the spaceship and take off again, I'll be able to use telepathy to find and read Tele's mind. And, once I can read it, we'll know where he is.'

We all agreed it might work. Freeze was particularly delighted, running over to All Powers and embracing her in an ice-cold hug.

'Thanks,' she said, wriggling free of him. 'But I don't think it'll work if I have brain freeze.'

We left the small platform of ice and started circling Earth, All Powers sat up the front with Lava, her eyes closed, deep in concentration.

After a while we heard her say, 'I know where he is.'

Freeze stood up excitedly and we had to restrain him from giving All Powers another brain-freezing hug.

All Powers still had her eyes closed. 'And there are other people on Earth!' she excitedly announced.

'What can you see?' Wolf was the first to ask.

'A fire with some people. Some are young, some are older, and they have hair and clothes and they are smiling and talking.'

'Where are they?' asked Lava.

'On land, obviously,' All Powers replied slowly, 'and I can see they're high up. On some kind of mountain. Or maybe it's a volcano.'

'Now we're talking!' exclaimed Lava excitedly, pressing the accelerator button. She turned and smiled at Obsidian. 'Did you hear that, buddy? They've got volcanos on Planet Earth!'

We travelled above miles and miles of blue water, going so fast that it didn't take us long to find what appeared to be the only island on the planet.

'It *is* a volcano,' Lava confirmed. 'Look at the circular ridge at the top. That's the edge of the crater.'

Despite missing the superhero school, I felt excited now, too. I reached down to pick up Fiver and hold him up to the window. As we approached the crater, I remembered the ones that Fiver and I visited and blasted on our little moon. This one was much bigger. Fiver barked at the thought of all the mischief we could get up to here and started licking my face affectionately.

Of course, the sight of a spaceship landing on the volcano was a big event for the few people who lived on Earth. That they weren't scared was testament to the stories that Tele must have told them. Whilst the people of Earth might have looked apprehensive as we disembarked our spaceship, they knew we weren't there to hurt them.

There were about twenty of them standing in a group by the fire. One of them stepped forward to greet us and there was something familiar about him. It was Tele. Still wearing his blue uniform but looking slightly different. Slightly healthier and more substantial. Freeze ran forward towards his friend.

Tele smiled brightly at him. 'Thank you,' he said.

'No problem,' replied Freeze. 'You made it, then?'

'Did you ever doubt me?'

All Powers had now joined them. 'Thank you for what, exactly?'

Freeze looked down at the ground awkwardly.

'He helped me, that's all,' murmured Tele.

Freeze lifted his head and looked at All Powers. 'I acted as decoy,' he told her. 'I froze myself deliberately so that Tele could get away.'

For a moment All Powers looked cross. But her frown quickly changed into a smile. 'I had my suspicions,' she said.

Freeze laughed. 'I couldn't believe you thought I'd be dumb enough to freeze myself anyway.' He turned to Tele. 'Come here,' he said, opening his arms. 'Give me a hug!'

It was a short hug – with Freeze anything other than a short hug could result in hypothermia – and once Tele had extricated himself from Freeze's grasp, Freeze said, 'You do feel different. You feel more, how can I put this? You feel more *here*.'

'There's a reason for that,' said Tele, cryptically. 'Come and join me and my new friends,' he made a gesture towards the people from Earth, who were starting to gather round us inquisitively. 'We can sit round the campfire and I'll tell you all about it. But be careful,' he continued. 'Planet Earth is dangerous right now. We must be vigilant at all times.'

CHAPTER 21

MARKIAN'S STORY

We sat around the fire and I looked at the faces of the people of Earth. Their life was how my life used to be: stuck on a rock with a crater. But their crater was bigger, and they had each other. There were twenty-one of them, I could now see. Some old, some just children, some in between. And they smiled at each other as they pointed at each of us in turn, finding humour, no doubt, in our appearance. What a motley crew we looked! They were particularly taken with Fiver. The fact that they knew how to act with him – how to stroke him, how to pick him up, how to throw sticks for him – made me feel that there had once been dogs on Earth too.

Before he started his story, Tele asked Obsidian, Laser and Lava to face away from the fire and keep guard over us.

'My name is Markian,' he began, looking over to where I was sitting. 'Like you were Mark before Lightning, I was Markian before Tele. Now I am Markian once more.

'The journey to Earth was my most challenging teleportation ever. The professor was right about that. One hundred galaxies *is* a very long distance to travel. So many wrong turns you can take. So much time you can waste. That's why it took me almost a day to get here!

'As I was teleporting, I held in my mind's eye images of people, people like us, people I imagined would live on Earth. That's a trick I'd practised a lot at school. Holding an image in my mind and imagining it so strongly that it eventually becomes real. But the problem was my image wasn't quite right.

'My imagination must have been close enough though, because I finally arrived here. In this place that they call The Last Place on Earth.

'The people were scared of me at first. I looked different from them because at that time I was still Tele – still partially transparent, still not quite here. But the people of Earth are peaceful; I could see that, and they welcomed me as one of their own, giving me food and shelter. And we sat around the campfire like friends.

'They told me their story. About how there had been a climate catastrophe on Earth. About how the ice had melted, the rain had come down and the land was covered by sea. They told me that they had travelled here to this volcano because it was a safe place and how they feared they were the last people alive.

'I asked them about the golden disc. Most of them had never heard of it, but some of the older ones had. They said it had been sent out to space years and years ago, as a way of making contact with people from other planets. I asked them if the golden disc had been a cry for help. They told me they didn't think so, but they were glad I was here because they certainly needed help now!

'I started telling them about my life. How I'd once been Markian but that my parents had spotted my talent for teleportation from an early age and how they'd eventually sent me away to superhero school. I told them about you all, about how amazing you were, how you'd be joining us soon and about how together we could help them.

'They were particularly interested in you, Freeze. They said that you could help them cool the Earth down, freeze some of the water to ice, make the land return. I said you could definitely do that. My best friend could do anything!

'Then one night, when we were sat round the fire, it all went wrong. I was listening to the girl over there talking about her journey to the volcano, when I was pulled from behind and dragged into the bushes. It happened so quickly that no one noticed I was gone. Before I could gather my thoughts enough to disappear, I felt a massive jaw clamping around my neck and big white teeth piercing my not-quite-there skin.

'I must have passed out. When I woke it was morning. I was lying amongst the bushes feeling very strange, as if I wasn't myself anymore. As if I wasn't Tele.

'I sat up and patted my head. I felt the dried blood and closed-up holes on my sore neck, the muscles of my thighs beneath my blue uniform. And I remembered what it had felt like to be a young boy. I remembered what it had been like before I started practising teleportation. What it felt like to have a real body. A solid body. I remembered what it felt like to be Markian.

'I joined my new friends and they could tell something had happened to me too. They were concerned and gave me jars of brightly coloured medicine. I said I was fine. That in a way I felt more myself than ever before!

'But there was one more thing I needed to know about my new self. And so, that night, before we sat down round the campfire, I stood by the crater of the volcano and closed my eyes. I held the image of the campfire in my mind and willed myself to teleport there. Nothing happened. I stayed at the top of the volcano. My powers gone. I was not Tele anymore. Tele was gone. Now I was truly Markian.

'And do you know what the funny thing was? I felt relieved.'

THE HUNT FOR CROCODILE

No one spoke for a while. I was the one to finally break the silence.

'I know exactly how you feel, Markian,' I said sympathetically. 'Becoming a superhero, becoming your power, means you lose touch with who you really are.'

Markian looked over at me and smiled. 'Thanks, Lightning,' he said. 'I mean, Mark.'

'Or, whatever!' I smiled in response.

'That's all well and good,' said All Powers, adopting a business-like tone, 'and we can think about that later, and even talk to the professor about it, but now is the time to prioritise. And our priority must be to find out who did this to Tele – I mean Markian – and stop them from doing it to the rest of us too. If whoever it is wanted to extract Tele's power, you can be sure they will want to extract the powers from the rest of us too.'

I'm pretty sure I wasn't the only one who was thinking what I was thinking at that moment. From Markian's description of what had happened to him, it was possible that his assailant had been none other than Crocodile. Dragging him over into the bushes. Clamping his neck in his great jaws. Extracting his power of teleportation with his sharp, white teeth.

But Crocodile here? On Planet Earth? Why would he travel all this way? Not to meet a crew of new superheroes, surely? And how had he burst through the ring of fire? It just didn't make any sense...

All Powers said she'd try telepathy again, but without knowing her enemy this proved impossible. Obsidian seemed pretty intent on pounding around with his massive stone body, jumping up and down and almost causing an earthquake, squashing the life out of anything and everything he came across.

But, collectively, we were at a loss. Fiver did his best to bring us together, running around and brushing up against all our legs, but it was no use. Weeks of practising for this moment and now we were drawing a blank. None us, not even All Powers, knew what to do next.

It was Wolf who broke our awkward silence. 'I could try smelling our enemy out,' he said.

'Really?' exclaimed Banana. 'You can do that?'

'I could,' he said tentatively, 'and you could all follow me, but it might not work.'

'It's the best idea we've got,' said All Powers decisively.

Some of the people from Earth wanted to come with us and so did Markian, but this wasn't a time to take chances. 'You stay here by the fire and look after them, Markian,' All Powers said, taking Markian to one side.

Remembering how sure of himself he had always been at school, I expected Markian to disobey All Powers, so I was surprised when he led the people of Earth back to the campfire. I began to think about how Markian and Tele were really very different people and I wondered if the same could be said about me. Tele was all about testing his powers, showing off to himself and to his friends. Markian seemed more understated and caring. What was Mark like? Was he also very different from Lightning?

'Someone should stay here,' Wolf suggested, looking at All Powers. 'To protect Markian and the people of Earth.'

'No,' said All Powers, having by now fully recovered her power of leadership. 'Our enemy is not interested in them. Our enemy is only interested in taking our superhero powers. We've got a better chance if we stick together.'

'Are you sure?' Wolf asked, looking at All Powers beseechingly with his jet black eyes.

'I'm sure.'

Wolf lowered himself to the ground and began sniffing. We followed him in single file up towards the crater of the volcano, Fiver's tail wagging all the way and Obsidian bringing up the rear as our massive impenetrable shield.

Progress was slow. Wolf made a great fuss about his sniffing, saying he wasn't sure he was picking up any scents. He kept stopping and standing up, saying he wasn't sure about this and that maybe we should just return to the spaceship and go home.

'Just do your best,' All Powers kept telling him.

'I said we couldn't rely on him,' said Obsidian unhelpfully.

Eventually we reached the top of the volcano and I could feel the electricity tingling in my fingers. Fiver jumped up and down expectantly at my side.

Wolf turned to the group, stood up and shrugged his shoulders, as if to say he wasn't sure if this was the place.

He walked over to me and, placing his mouth again my ear, he whispered, 'I'm so sorry, Mark.'

I was confused. I didn't know what he meant. Sorry? Sorry for what? Before I had a chance to ask, a man – a typical man at first sight, but a man who, I could now see, had so many teeth that it looked as if his mouth had been forced to lengthen – emerged from the depths of the crater.

THE BATTLE COMMENCES

That's what Crocodile looked like. A person of average height and build. Not really tall like Obsidian or Lava. Not steaming like Freeze or sharp and pointy like Laser. Not not-quite-here like Tele had been. Just ordinary.

Aside from that one key difference. Those large, pearly white teeth that were so big and so numerous that his mouth had been forced to become as long and wide as a Crocodile's to keep them all in.

I don't know whether he was always like that or, like Wolf, just when he was in fight mode. He didn't stick around for long enough for us to find out. And I never got to ask Wolf. What happened next was a blur.

Wolf was shouting at Crocodile, 'Not them. They're not the leaders!'

Crocodile's great jaws were snapping furiously as if this were irrelevant.

I could feel lightning surging in my fingertips. I would let him have it. I would destroy Crocodile and save the Alliance. Professor Banks would be so proud!

But before I could discharge – before I had a chance to blast the volcano's crater to smithereens, to send it collapsing around Crocodile, to trap him inside of the volcano for ever – I was knocked to the ground. Wolf was on top of me, rolling me down the side of the volcano and away from the others.

Fiver must have followed us. I could hear him barking

loudly. We came to a standstill by a cluster of rocks, Wolf pinning me down, his jet black eyes looking directly into my own.

I felt the lightning in my fingertips but I was reluctant to use it on my best friend. And besides, although Wolf was using his sinewy strength to make sure I didn't get back up again, I could tell from the look in his eyes that he wasn't going to hurt me.

'What are you doing?' I asked him, beyond confused by his actions. 'I thought you were my friend!'

'Just stay down. *Please*,' Wolf whispered in all seriousness. 'You have to trust me. Pretend that you're dead.'

Pretend I was dead? It made no sense. No sense at all. I couldn't work out what Wolf meant, why he was acting the way he was or why he'd been acting differently ever since the professor had shown us the golden disc. It wasn't just because my brain can be a little slow to process things sometimes. It was also because I could still hear the snapping of Crocodile's jaws.

'OK,' I told Wolf, realising the only way I could help the other superheroes would be to convince him to get off me.

'I'm sorry,' Wolf repeated, removing his claws from my chest and snaking his way towards the others who were fighting Crocodile at the crater's edge.

As soon as Wolf was off me, I stood up, Fiver barking wildly at my side. I felt the charge of electricity in my fingertips and instinctively wanted to set it free, to blast the crater from which Crocodile had emerged.

Up ahead, I could make out his great mouth snapping wildly. It was a savage sight. He was outnumbered, but his flailing jaws made it difficult for any of the crew to get near him. The steadfast Freeze was flung to one side as Crocodile's jaws cracked into his arm. Then Laser was knocked down as the jaws smashed onto his head. Then, amongst this ocean of fury, I saw Obsidian striding out towards him.

'Bite on this!' Obsidian shouted, thrusting his fist inside Crocodile's mouth.

Crocodile bit down hard. The sound of his mighty teeth crunching against the arm of the strongest-ever superhero was one that chilled me to my bones. Screeching and cracking, as if the planet itself had been split in two.

To give him his dues, Crocodile didn't even whimper. There was blood around his mouth and teeth were scattered on the floor like glistening white pebbles, but I think he still believed that with just one more bite he could extract Obsidian's powers.

Crocodile didn't get the chance, though. Before he could bring his jaws down on Obsidian's arm again, Laser had found his marble-like eyes with his own. He must have had his lasers on maximum power, because smoke started coming from Crocodile's eyes almost immediately and an acrid burning smell filled the air.

Again, Crocodile let out not one whimper. Not a single cry. He kept going with his preferred weapon, snapping his jaws wildly, blinded by his desire to get our powers. But his jaws were only biting the air.

By this time, Wolf had reached the others. Before I could think to call out to warn them, he had jumped swiftly on Laser, knocking him to the ground.

Laser disarmed, Wolf ran to the edge of the crater and stood up on two legs in front of Crocodile.

A part of me was still expecting Wolf to jump on him, to pin Crocodile down and rip flesh from his bones. Everything had happened so fast that I still hadn't worked out what was really going on. So, when Wolf opened his arms to

Crocodile, held him tightly and wiped the blood from Crocodile's eyes and mouth with the hairy backs of his hands, it was a great shock.

'What are you doing, Wolf?' cried Laser, standing up and brushing the dust from his blue uniform.

'Finish him off, Wolf!' bellowed Obsidian.

'He's a traitor!' shouted Lava. 'I always knew he was one of them.'

All Powers held up her arms and stepped forwards. 'Tell them, Wolf,' she commanded. 'Tell them why you won't destroy Crocodile.'

Wolf shook his head slowly. He placed his mouth up against the side of Crocodile's head. He was telling him something. Something that none of us could hear.

Wolf sunk to the ground and, with a mighty leap, hurled himself towards All Powers.

CHAPTER 24

WHAT HAPPENED TO CROCODILE

Banana was the first to react, hurling a vine around Wolf's back. This restricted Wolf but he still had All Powers pinned to the ground. Then Lava opened her mouth, carefully aiming a stream of lava at Wolf's tail.

'Enough!' I shouted, unable to bear the sight of my friend experiencing so much pain. 'Crocodile's the one we should be fighting.'

I ran to the edge of the volcano but could see no sign of him. Fiver was barking louder than ever, jumping up and down. The tingling in my fingertips was now so strong that, before I could think better of it, I lifted my hands in the air and sent my lightning flashing across the crater and into the rocks on the other side.

It created an almighty impact. Much greater than any I'd managed before. The whole far side of the crater collapsed and fell into the volcano. Within seconds of the rock hitting the bottom, plumes of smoke and rock dust rose into the air, engulfing us all and sending us sprawling to the ground, coughing, choking and rubbing our eyes.

Later that day, when we were back in the spaceship, Lava said she'd thought that I'd made the volcano erupt. What happened to Crocodile? None of us can say for sure. He'd been badly injured. His teeth broken, his eyes scarred, but he might have managed to get away when Wolf distracted us by attacking All Powers.

How far could he have gone, though, in such a state? Could a seriously wounded Crocodile really have made it back to Dark Planet?

And then there was my impulsive act of destruction. If Crocodile had been making his escape, wouldn't the collapse of the volcano's crater have stopped him in his tracks? Surely, he would have been pulled to his death, smashed to smithereens beneath the rubble.

I don't know the answers to these questions. I don't know anyone who does.

All I do know is that we never saw Crocodile again. Even now that Dark Planet has joined the Alliance, no one there has been able to provide any convincing evidence that Crocodile ever returned.

CHAPTER 25 LEAVING EARTH

To be fair to Wolf, he didn't try to escape under the cloud of smoke. When the dust finally settled, we saw him just sat there, looking dejected and refusing to speak.

Obsidian picked him up and, with the agreement of All Powers, took him to the spaceship where he bound him in chains.

Some of the others wanted to take revenge and finish Wolf off there and then. I'm sure you can guess who they were. They said they'd always thought Wolf was from Dark Planet. They'd always known he wasn't one of us.

It was a difficult time for us all. None of us knew just how wide-reaching the repercussions of that day would be in the end.

But, as with most things, All Powers had the final word. 'We'll take him back to the professor. We will let her decide.' With that, she took it upon herself to reconnect the communication system and radioed the professor to apologise on behalf of us all. She let her know that we would soon be returning to school with Wolf as a prisoner.

I felt numb. My best friend in all the galaxies had betrayed us. My best friend was in alliance with Crocodile. It was too much for me to take in. I couldn't believe what was happening.

We returned to the campfire and, once again, All Powers did the talking. She explained what had happened with Crocodile and the volcano. She explained how we had been betrayed by Wolf.

Markian said he had never quite trusted him. 'He was the one who deciphered the golden disc and brought us here. He must have known that Crocodile would be waiting for us.'

'There's a lot we still don't know,' said All Powers. 'And now's not the time for speculation. Now's the time for us to leave.'

She addressed the people of Earth and said how it would be a pleasure if they would join the Alliance. How we would send another mission shortly to help them save their watery planet.

'That's a great offer, but there's something you should know,' said Freeze, standing up and walking over to where Markian was sat. 'Do you want to tell them or shall I?' he asked him.

Markian looked at All Powers and then at each of us in turn. His eyes had misted over slightly, as if he were about to cry. Markian really was a very different person from Tele.

'I'm going to stay here,' Markian said eventually. 'I feel more at home here than I've felt in a long time. And besides, the superhero school is no place for me now that I no longer have a power.'

We tried our best to talk him out of it. Maybe his power would come back. Or another power would replace it. But none of us really believed that. I suppose all of us knew that it was no use. Markian had already made his mind up.

What happened next was an even greater surprise.

'And I'm staying too,' said Freeze quietly, a tiny frozen tear already formed in the corner of one of his eyes. 'Markian is my friend and the people of Earth need me. I can be of great service here.'

It's widely known what happened to Earth next. How its ecosystems were restored. How the ice caps reformed and how the land returned. And that's all thanks to Freeze. A legend beyond legends! A kind hero who dedicated his life to saving Earth and its people.

As we waved goodbye to them from our spaceship, all of us superheroes, Wolf included, were in tears.

CHAPTER 26 WOLF SPEAKS

The journey home was a sad one. The worst thing was, we should have been happy. We had defeated Crocodile. Our young, naïve and motley crew had probably rid the universe of its arch enemy – or so we thought at the time – making the galaxies a safer place to roam.

But for everything we had gained, we had also lost a lot. Tele had lost his powers and was now Markian, and Freeze had stayed on Earth with him. Wolf had betrayed me and the rest of the crew and was bound in chains at the back of our spaceship. We spent the journey snapping at each other, blaming each other quite irrationally for what had happened. Not even All Power's skill of diplomacy or Fiver's friendliness could help us with that. Obsidian was especially grumpy now that he didn't have Freeze to help him cool Lava's continual outpourings.

Towards the end of our journey, whilst I was bringing him his lunch, Wolf spoke to me. 'I need to explain what happened,' he said simply.

'Haven't you let everyone, me included, down enough?' I replied unhappily.

But I let the others know what he'd said. They felt the same way as me and didn't think Wolf would tell the truth, anyway. But, as always, All Powers had the final word. 'It might do us all good to hear what Wolf has to say.'

I went to fetch Wolf, gripping hold of the backs of the seats to hold myself down. It didn't seem right for him to tell his story while bound in chains, so I freed him, but gripped his arm tightly with one hand whilst keeping us anchored by holding the back of the seat with my other hand. I wanted Wolf to feel the hurt he had caused me. But slowly my grip softened. I led him to the seat next to mine in the centre of the spaceship and instructed him to fasten himself in.

No one questioned what I'd done. The sad look in Wolf's eyes meant none of us believed he would try to attack us now.

'I *do* come from Dark Planet,' Wolf began. 'I know what you've all been taught about Crocodile, but I urge you to believe me when I say that almost none of it is true.

'Crocodile was a good leader. He is respected by most of Dark Planet's people. He wasn't interested in taking the powers from the few people that had them. Rather, he was intent in developing them for the good of the planet. I am a prime example of this. Crocodile noticed my wolfish tendencies at a young age and took a special interest in me. He taught me how to control my natural urges, how to be human and then how to become a wolf. To become a wolf who could hunt for food.

'The only time he used his bite to take powers away was when one of his people committed a crime against others. Of course, there were times when people disagreed with the nature of the justice he handed out. Some said that the person was actually innocent; others complained that the punishment was too harsh. But that was the extent of any bad feelings towards their leader. On the whole, Crocodile was much loved on our planet.

'When my parents were still young, Crocodile became interested in life beyond Dark Planet. He believed there were other planets out there and he wanted to visit them and find out about the people there. But our scientists weren't as sophisticated as yours – instead of travelling by spaceship, Crocodile had to make do with the superpowers of flight, taken from his own people. He took more and more, until one day he was strong enough to fly all the way to Red Planet.

'I can't stress this enough – Crocodile's intentions were wholly peaceful. But the people of Red Planet weren't to know this when they saw him approach. Soon after he landed at the foot of one of their many volcanos, Crocodile found some of their people standing before him.

'Now, what happened next is a matter of perspective. Of course, the people of Red Planet and, in turn, the people of your alliance, say that Crocodile attacked first. And Crocodile and the people of Dark Planet will say that it was the other way around and the people of Red Planet made the first move.

'Something I've come to learn over the past few months is that the truth is not as straightforward as history would have it seem. We were told by Crocodile that the people of the Alliance were evil and when the Alliance set up the superhero school and imprisoned Dark Planet in a ring of fire, it was proof to us that he was right! How else were the people of Dark Planet supposed to react but with violent indignation? How else were we supposed to view your superheroes but as evil oppressors!

'Now I know that is not wholly true. That all of you, and I include Obsidian and Lava in this, can be kind and thoughtful. But the same can be said of Crocodile.

'The idea of me joining you at the superhero school was, of course, Crocodile's. My name was Isaac, but as my wolfish tendencies grew he started calling me Wolf. He trained me to become my new name and he trained me in deceit as well.

He told me that if the scouts from the school picked me up they would interrogate me and ask me questions about Dark Planet. One wrong word and I would be killed, instantly.

'At the same time that he was training me, his scientists were beginning to develop spaceships that could penetrate the ring of fire. They planned to launch me up into space and leave me orbiting the superhero school. The scouts would find me and, seeing my wolfish powers, bring me to the school. If they suspected that I was from Dark Planet, I was to tell them they were being ignorant and that it wasn't only people from Dark Planet that had animal powers.

'On the day I was to leave, Crocodile told me the rest of the plan. He had a golden disc that had been sent from Planet Earth many years ago. He would send it back into space, towards the superhero school. When they found it, the professors would want to work out what it meant and would travel to Earth to encourage them to join the Alliance.

'Crocodile explained to me that this is where I came in. I would be the one to decipher the golden disc. I would explain it was a cry for help from Planet Earth and that the professors and the best superheroes need to go there.

'Of course, this didn't quite go as planned. Professor Banks fell for it. You all fell for it, so much so that you insisted on disobeying the professor and hatching a renegade mission yourselves. And once you were boarding the spaceship, there was no way I could let you go to Earth by yourselves.

'So that was the plan. A plan I found it difficult to carry out. I tried to keep my distance from all of you. I tried not to like you. Not to become your friends. But it was impossible.

'I know what you think about Crocodile. I understand why, as well. But try to see things from his point of view. His intentions were peaceful until his planet was imprisoned by the ring of fire. And even when he used me to lure you to Earth so he could extract your powers, he still wanted to spare your lives, just like he did with Tele. At least, that's what he told me.

'I know you hate me, but I'd grown up on Dark Planet. Grown up knowing the rest of the planets in the galaxies detested us. Had imprisoned us. Had taken away our intergalactic freedoms. Why wouldn't we strike back? Why shouldn't we take your powers and make Dark Planet strong again?'

CHAPTER 27
WOLF DISAPPEARES

No one spoke when Wolf had finished. Lava was shaking her head and Obsidian looked stonily into the distance. Wolf's story was difficult for me to comprehend. His version of events was so different from everything I'd been told, from everything I had wanted to believe. Wolf stood up and I led him to the back of the spaceship, binding him once again in the chains.

'I know it's a lot to ask, Mark,' he said to me quietly, 'but I think, one day, you of all people will understand.'

'What makes you think that?' I asked pointedly.

'You grew up on a moon with only a Fiver as a friend,' Wolf said. 'The first you'd heard of the Alliance and Dark Planet was when you arrived at the superhero school. Their version of history is not your version of history, Mark. That's why my version of history also deserves to be heard.'

I didn't respond at the time, but Wolf's plea stayed with me for the rest of the journey. When we got to the security circle there were officers waiting to take Wolf away.

That was the last time I ever saw him. Bound in chains, his head bowed, flanked by security officers. He turned round one last time and looked at me with his piercing jet black eyes.

The rest of us were met by the professor who sent us to our dorms without any dinner. Normal lessons were suspended. Over the next few days we were interviewed by the professor, one at a time.

I can't speak for the others – I can only guess what they told the professor – but I told her how conflicted Wolf had been ever since the golden disc appeared. About how reluctant he'd been to lead us up the volcano. About how he'd tried to spare me. How he'd tried to stop us from killing Crocodile. How he'd told his alternative history about why Crocodile wanted to extract our powers.

The professor looked at me, unable to hide her amazement at what I was saying. 'And do you believe him, Lightning?'

Did I believe him? I know the professor wanted me to say no. I know that given how he'd deceived us all, *no* would have been the most rational answer. *No* was, most probably, the answer some or most of the others had given her. But in my heart of hearts, I knew that *no* was the wrong answer.

'Yes,' I said, watching alarm spread across the professor's face, her glasses falling to the floor.

'And one other thing, Professor,' I added. 'From now on, please call me Mark.'

It took a while for my conversation with the professor to change anything. In fact, it probably wasn't my conversation with the professor that ultimately changed anything at all. If anyone should take the credit for making the Alliance see that the people of Dark Planet weren't evil after all, it was All Powers.

She's the most amazing superhero I've ever known! Her ability to see every situation from every perspective and then to take them all on board to know what should be done was, without a doubt, her most enviable power. Risking being kicked out of superhero school, it wasn't long after Wolf's disappearance that All Powers began her campaign to free the people of Dark Planet from the ring of fire. She put up posters all over the school, spoke passionately in sessions with the professors and persuaded the rest of us – not that I needed much persuading – to join her.

She then started asking the difficult questions we'd all left unspoken to those in authority. What had they done with Wolf? Was he imprisoned in the security circle? Had they killed him? Banished him into space?

No answers were forthcoming and over the years as we travelled the galaxies on missions that were never as eventful as our first, I began to accept the worst. That Wolf was, most probably, dead.

Slowly but surely, the changes came, culminating in the Alliance extinguishing the ring of fire. Superheroes, as you may know, retire young and by the time the fire was put out we were nearly ready to call it a day and either return to our homes or become professors. All Powers insisted that our crew's final mission should be to Dark Planet, to be the crew who made peace with them and asked their leader to join the Alliance. It would have made sense to have let us go, but I guess some of the powers-that-be didn't wholly trust us. They chose a younger crew, one that had less emotional baggage than we did, saying we were ready for retirement.

When their mission returned, we sat here in this lecture theatre as they told us that they had met the leader of Dark Planet and that they wanted to join the Alliance. I couldn't believe it when then told us that the leader was a man called Isaac, and that Isaac was none other than Wolf. He was still alive after all! The authorities had taken mercy on him and sent him back to Dark Planet. There, he'd been joyfully welcomed by people in need of a new leader.

It made my year. And here I am, a whole year later, standing in the same lecture theatre, welcoming the first recruits from Dark Planet to our superhero school. For a boy who grew up on a rock with a five-legged dog, I have to say this day by far exceeds anything I could have imagined! This is the happiest day of my life.

WOLF RETURNS

The lecture theatre was packed with students, professors and members of the Intergalactic Press. As soon as Professor Mark Wells had finished, they all rose, enthusiastic in their applause. The applause was so loud that the barks of the professor's old dog, Fiver, could not be heard.

The professor began to leave the stage. As he did, a man at the back of the lecture theatre started to make his way forward. His movements were slow, making him seem older than most of the people there. His hair was straggly and brown, and it covered his face.

At first the professor didn't notice the man. He had turned to pick up his dog when he was stopped by the touch of a hand on his shoulder.

'Mark,' the man said. 'I always knew you were a true superhero. I always knew you'd see things from my perspective.'

The professor turned around in amazement. The man standing in front of him was hunched and older than he could have imagined. His brown hair now flecked with grey. As the man brushed his hair back to reveal his jet black eyes, the professor started to speak... He stopped himself, appearing to change his mind.

'Isaac,' he said eventually, tears forming in the corners of his eyes. 'This truly is the happiest day of my life!'

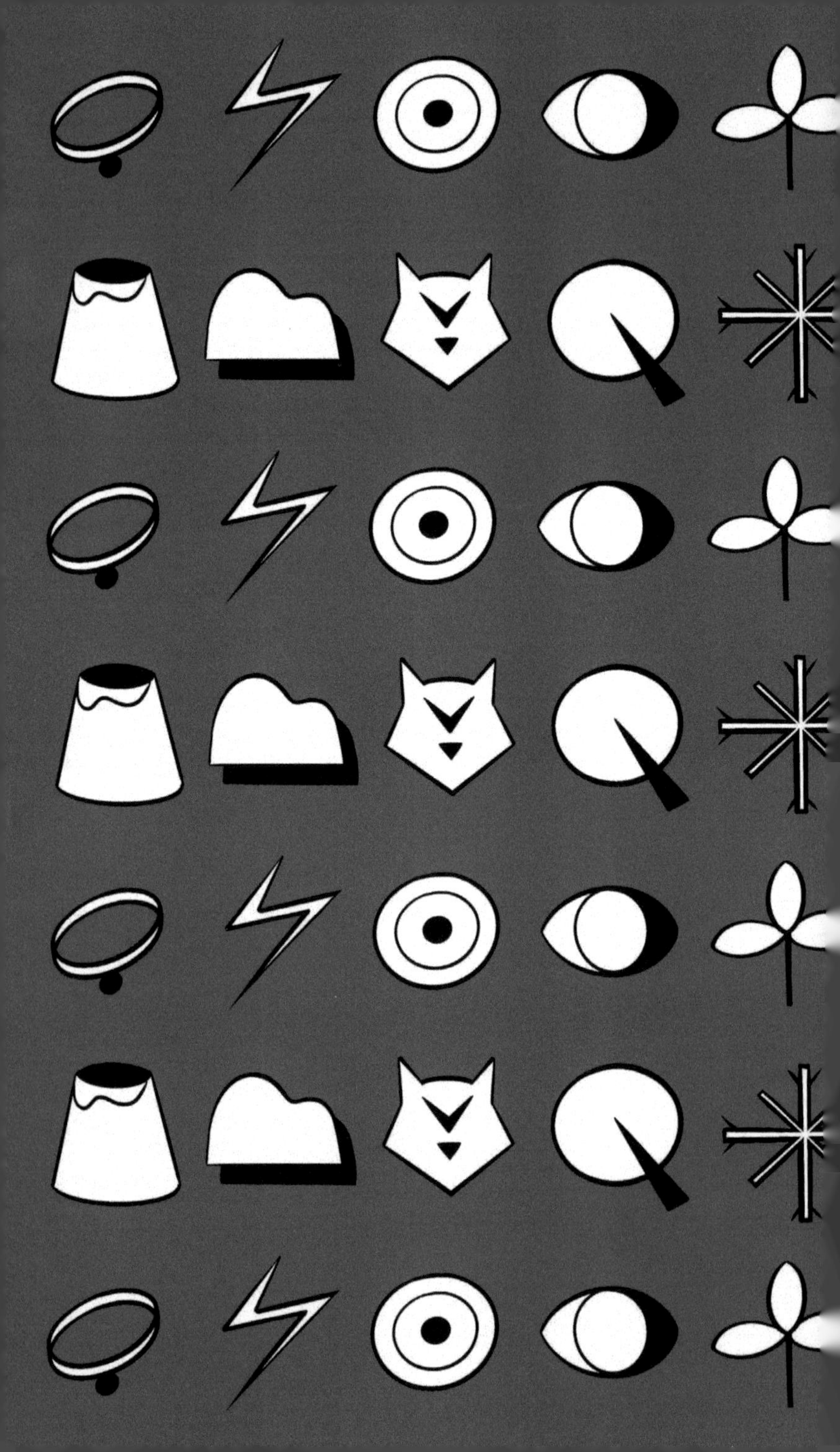